THE AUDACITY TO SAY YOU LOVE ME

TERUKA B.

The Audacity To Say You Love Me

Mailing List

To stay up to date on new releases, plus get information on contests, sneak peeks, and more,

Go To The Website Below...

www.colehartsignature.com

ACKNOWLEDGMENTS

First and foremost, I would like to give all praise to God, my leader, my father. Without his love none of this would be possible. There is no me without you.

Kisses, love, and hugs to all my supporters. My day ones that have been following me since I came into this literary world in 2008. I want you all to know just how much I appreciate your continued support over the years.

To my beloved loved ones that have been supportive through this journey, I couldn't ask for better love in my life. Tijah, Kevin Ji'haud, Karleyah and Shelli Marie: You all mean so much to me and I wouldn't trade you guys for nothing in this world! I love y'all immensely.

Lastly, to the friends I grew up with in this small city. Thank y'all so much!

CHAPTER ONE

"Girl, thank you so much for coming to get me from the airport. I have been blowing Deion up since last night to remind him," Indya told Mariah as she got in the car after putting her daughter, Gianna, in her car seat. "I would have had my whip, but Deion insisted on dropping me off."

"Now you know that it's not a problem. But let's be real for a minute, you need to leave his tired ass alone. Every time you need him, he's always MIA or too busy. Knowing him, he's probably laid the fuck up. How many times are you going to let him play in your face, Indya?" Mariah scolded.

"Mariah, I can respect what you're saying, but Deion loves me. He knows the next time he tries that cheating shit I'm out! And Gianna is coming with me."

"You been saying that for the last four years and nothing has changed. Y'all have been engaged since you had Gianna and he still hasn't picked a damn date. Girl, you need to wake up," Mariah spoke honestly. That was her bestie and all, but she needed to hear the truth from someone, especially since her family acted like the shit was normal. What kind of mother tells their child to stick around because they had overcome so many other issues and she could tell he loved her?

Indya wasn't about to argue with her friend because she was right. She loved Deion more than she loved herself. When they first got together, she thought having his one and only daughter would change him, but that only seemed to make it worse.

"Thank you again, girl," Indya recited as they pulled up to the house she and Deion shared. She got her baby girl out the back seat and waved her friend off.

"I'm not going nowhere until you make it inside. Look, that nigga's car right there! Why the hell he not answering your calls?" Indya ignored her and proceeded into the house. Right away she was hit in the face with slow music blasting from their spare bedroom. She laid her daughter on the couch while she slept.

I know this nigga ain't doing this shit! she thought.

Getting closer to the room, she heard Deion's voice as clear as day. Her heart sank to the bottom of her stomach. She grabbed the mace from her purse and got it ready.

"Yeah, just like that, bae. I'm about to cum. Shit," he moaned with each thrust. Deion grabbed her by the back of her hair and smacked her ass.

"Oh Deion, I love daddy's dick," she moaned. "Cum in this pussy, baby."

Indya wanted to sit there longer but she would be damned if she was about to let them finish. She kicked the door in with force.

"Oh shit!" he yelled, pushing Tyra over while trying to pull his pants up.

Indya's mind went blank, and she sprayed them both down with the mace. She tried to go beat up the girl that he was fuckin' but she started choking right along with them.

"What in the hell, Deion! Who is that?" Tyra asked as she scrambled around on the floor.

Indya couldn't believe that she had tried spraying them and got fucked up in the process. She ran outside for some air when Mariah jumped out the car.

"What the fuck is going on?"

"That motherfuck—that nigga," she stammered, still trying to breathe. "I need some water."

"Bitch, what?!" Mariah asked, getting pissed by the second. She snatched a bottle of water out the front of the car and poured it all over her face.

Surprisingly, soon as Indya got herself back together, the girl nor Deion still hadn't come out the house.

"That motherfucker got some bitch in my house! I'm gone kill his ass!" she screamed.

"Oh, hell nah! Let's go beat her ass," Mariah told her as she made her way into the house.

"Nope, wait until she come outside. I got something for her ass. Grab the water hose."

"Girl, what in the hell is a damn water hose going to do?"

"Just do it," she instructed.

No sooner than she told her that, Tyra came out the house creeping.

"Now!" Mariah turned the water on full blast and sprayed her all in the face and body. Indya took that time to run up on her. She hit her with blow after blow, sending her crashing into the ground. Indya was surprised that she was keeping up with her.

"Beat her ass, Indya!!" Mariah cheered her friend on as she turned the water to the hose off.

"Y'all chill, man!" Deion barked, running out the house with nothing but basketball shorts on.

"Step the fuck back before I spray your triflin' ass too!" Mariah warned.

"Fuck you, whore!" He quickly grabbed Indya off Tyra, giving her time to get to the other side of the street to get into her vehicle, but not before Mariah sprayed them both again for good measure.

Indya kicked and screamed for Deion to let her go to no avail. "Let me go, you bastard!"

"If I let you go, will you chill out? I love you! Just let me explain."

The audacity to say you love me.

"Yeah, I'm good," she lied. Soon as he let her go, she attacked him.

Fed up a with seeing her friend make a fool out of herself, Mariah pulled Indya off him.

"Chill, boo. This nigga not even worth it. Y'all neighbors are looking and recording shit!" she told her. "Mind yawls damn business!"

"Let me explain, baby. It's not what you think," he pleaded. "Come on, let's go inside and talk."

Indya gave her friend that look of embarrassment and without another word, Mariah got in her Tahoe and drove off. By the time they were about to go back into the house, Gianna was peering at them rubbing her eyes.

"Mommy, potty."

"You lucky my baby needs me," she huffed with a wide grin, picking their baby up. She took her to the bathroom and headed to the master room.

"Baby, I know you're mad at me, but just give me the chance to explain."

"Deion, do you really think this shit will always be enough for me? I mean," she laughed. "I mean, at what point will you realize that I won't be here forever?" She was beyond disgusted with him.

"I know you won't be here if I keep fuckin' up. Shorty offered me three racks to knock her off," he lied.

"I don't give a damn if she offered your ass the kingdom of heaven! You don't do that shit! Do me and Gianna mean anything to you?!" she shouted as tears poured heavily down her cheeks.

"Baby, I just need to go get some bread up. I'm thinking about going out to Greensboro for a few weeks to help my boy out with some shit he got going on. I'm trying to make some real bread with a nigga I trust. We about to lose this house!" he lied. Truth was he just needed to get away from her for a while. Over the past six months she hadn't touched him. It could have been because of the way he had been moving lately, but he wasn't completely sure. He just needed a break from Indya and her controlling ways.

Although Deion was a licensed real estate agent and Indya was junior attorney at the law firm she worked for part time, the money was never enough, especially since Deion had her spoiled with lavish things. Besides that, their house was keeping them on the not-so-rich list. Their mortgage payment was ridiculous.

"Deion, you're not leaving this fuckin' house because of some bullshit! Wanting to leave when you know this relationship is in jeopardy is insane!" She laughed crazily, walking off.

"Don't give me that shit, Indya! These niggas out here be gatekeeping. We need this money!" Deion complained.

"What happened to them niggas you used to run with?"

"You know I don't fuck with Gates like that no more. That means his boys are cut too." Deion had to cut them off because they were in too deep. He was just there for extra cash but that was their career, so they moved differently than he did.

"I told ya ass to stop that gambling shit when we moved in this fuckin' house, but your hardheaded ass don't listen! You're so selfish! What about our savings?" she huffed.

"Man, that shit is gone," he honestly spoke, lowering his head in shame.

"Are you fuckin' kidding me, Deion! That was to keep us afloat! I cannot believe you done blew our savings on your gambling mess! Obviously, your ass doesn't know what you're doing, buddy. Give it the fuck up! I am so sick of this shit!"

"I know I fucked up baby, but please just let me go make this right," he pleaded.

"Why can't he just come out here? Greensboro is basically next door. You know what? Leave and we won't be here when you get back!" she threatened, storming off to their bedroom.

Deion honestly didn't care what she chose to do, but he knew that she wasn't going anywhere. If the constant cheating didn't run her off, she was as good as locked in forever, so her tantrum wouldn't last long. He would leave out the following day.

"Ugh, get it out of me," she panted.

"Come on Thyri, push girl," her best friend Kamari coached. "She's almost out. You got this boo."

"Shut the fuck up and stop rubbing my damn shoulders," she spat, fidgeting around in the bed. Although she'd been through childbirth before, Thyri could never get used to that pain.

This was the third birth that Thyri had to endure without the joy of being an actual mother. Each time she delivered a baby with her boyfriend Kane, the state took them away from her. She gave birth to her first baby girl at only fifteen years old while she was still in foster care. After she was snatched from her arms, Thyri was never the same. Her life never seemed to be complete.

Thyri had extreme abandonment issues, so when she met Kane, she attached herself to him and his past trauma issues. They met the day of her seventeenth birthday and had been stuck like glue since that day. He was the definition of toxic and a born narcissist, but she loved him. Although the bad outweighed the good, Thyri hung onto the good things about him and refused to let go.

Kane and Thyri had a very tumultuous relationship and everyone in Greensboro knew it. There was no hiding their relationship because it stayed on social media as well. They basically made one another look completely ignorant and like a joke to anyone on the outside looking into their relationship. It never mattered how embarrassing it was, she stood by her man through whatever.

Kane wasn't going anywhere anytime soon. In the past she made attempts to leave him, but he would come back and sweep her off her feet again. After a few days things would go back to normal with them fighting like cats and dogs.

"Oh my God! I'm never doing this shit again," she whimpered, pushing as hard as she could.

Feeling relieved and a thousand pounds lighter, Thyri gave her baby girl life and fell backward. She rested her head on the flat hospital pillow, exhausted.

"You did it, boo. She's so pretty. Looking as chocolate as Kane with y'all pretty ass hair," Kamari told her, gazing at the beautiful bundle of joy.

Thyri sat up a little bit after relaxing for a hot second. "Can I hold her?" she requested, holding her hands out.

"I'm sorry, Ms. Jacobs, we cannot allow you to bond with her," the nurse stated, passing Thyri's baby girl to a social worker.

Although she knew what to expect, it still hurt her to the core that she couldn't have all her children under the same roof because of the bullshit she had been dealing with for years. There was nothing she could do but sob as they cleaned her. Kamari tried her best to soothe her friend, but it wasn't an easy task.

Soon as Thyri got pregnant with this baby, Kamari questioned her as to why she hadn't gotten an abortion or even gotten her tubes tied yet. Thyri let her friend know that even though she didn't have her babies, she had high hopes in getting them back, getting married to the man of her dreams, and having more babies for him. She wanted better for her children, and deep down she knew that God would give her the family that she so desperately craved to have with Kane.

Thyri cried so many dreadful, heartbreaking tears because she was hopeful that this time things would be different. The more she hoped for the best, it seemed as if things stayed the same.

Kamari had been her best friend since they first met her first year of middle school, so she was going to ride for her friend through whatever. She stood by her bedside and held her friend while she cried, trying her best to keep her in good spirits. She just didn't want her to keep having these kids by this man that couldn't care less about her or their children's wellbeing.

Three days later Thyri was released from the hospital. Kamari came to pick her up with a bouquet of flowers, a bottle of Hennessey, and a big teddy bear to congratulate her.

"Girl, you didn't have to do all of this for me. Thank you," Thyri spoke with a wide smile.

"I love ya ass and I know how you been hurting behind everything, so it's only right I do something special for you," she replied. "You deserve it, boo. We know Kane's leeching ass ain't gone do shit special for you! Whew, let me stop." The hate that Kamari had in her heart for Kane was so strong that she couldn't even stand speaking on him. Everything about him irritated her soul.

"I hope you know you're drinking this shit with me. I am not trying to drink all this alone."

"No ma'am, I got to head to work after I drop you at the crib. I wish I could though," Kamari explained.

"Well, I'll just save it until you get off then, heffa," Thyri replied, pouting.

"I'm so sorry boo, but I have to pull a double tonight and tomorrow night at the hospital."

"Ugh, you suck! Guess I'll be getting drunk all by myself then."

"Girl, bye! You know damn well Kane about to be right at the crib when you get there." Kamari laughed. She couldn't stand the ground that man walked on but she remained cordial for her friend.

"Don't remind me, girl. That sorry bastard could have at least come to the hospital with me or called me. I haven't heard from his ass at all, and he hasn't answered his phone," she huffed.

"You been knowing that nigga wasn't shit, boo. You need to leave his ass alone and make him get up out ya shit," Kamari scolded.

"I know, girl. I'm just waiting for the right time because I know it won't be as simple as saying get out and he'll leave," Thyri explained as they pulled up to her building. "You know it isn't that easy."

"Yeah, I can't imagine." Of course, Kamari wanted to say more, but she just let it go because it was a pointless venture.

They'd had that conversation way too many times and it went in one ear and out the other. All she could do was be there to pick up the pieces when it was all said and done.

"Thank you so much, boo. I can't thank you enough for everything. Fuck a nigga. You're my fuckin' rock," she spoke, leaning toward her friend for a hug.

Once they hugged, Thyri got out the car and dreadfully headed to her apartment. No sooner than she put her key in the door, Kane snatched it open.

"Damn nigga, I thought ya ass was dead," she harshly spoke, rolling her eyes and walking past him. "Couldn't find ya ass for days and you're just in my shit kickin' it!" She shook her head and went inside.

"My bad, baby. I lost my shit," he told her. "I love you."

"Yeah, okay Kane. Anyway, I got this bottle my girl got me. Do you wanna drink this shit with me?" She didn't have the energy to argue with him.

Thyri didn't wanna be bothered but she knew that he wouldn't be leaving anytime soon, and she needed a drink, so why not?

Not even halfway through the bottle, Kane was trying to fuck. He knew she couldn't, but he didn't care. The second Thyri pushed him away, he got mad and beat her ass down, sending her right back to the hospital and landing himself in jail because the neighbor called the police on him...

CHAPTER TWO

Thyri had been living her best life since Kane got locked up because it not only allowed her to get him away from her, but she was also able to get a restraining order on him after that as well. Knowing her weakness for Kane, Thyri was glad that a neighbor had saved her the trouble by calling the police on him.

She had to be honest with herself because she did love that man with everything inside of her, but it was time. Hell, it was well overdue that she got rid of him once and for all.

Of course, he bonded out of jail the next day, and the restraining order for sure didn't keep him from trying to contact her daily. It had been a little over a week and Thyri was proud of herself for not giving in to him like all the other times. She constantly forgave him and never held him accountable. This time she was moving differently, not posting her business on social media as much, and being calm.

Deep in her thoughts, Thyri wished that she had her kids right by her side because they meant the world to her. She was tired of drowning her sorrows with weed and drinks every day.

Thyri had graduated from Virginia College a few months

before she got pregnant with her last baby girl. She found a job in her field at the hospital alongside Kamari.

She was a medical assistant and Kamari was an LPN. Thyri was also working at Texas Roadhouse part time. Her time always seemed spent on work and not much downtime. Sometimes it was overwhelming, but she kept pushing. Although she worked both jobs part time, she made sure her weekends were free.

Thyri got up and headed for the shower. It was her day off and she planned on getting her nails and feet done. She hardly ever treated herself, but she vowed to do it more often because self-care was important for mental health. It would be a lot easier now since her baby daddy wasn't in her face asking for money to flip every five minutes and Kane wasn't the kind of guy that you could just say no to.

As soon as she turned the water on someone started beating on her door, scaring her half to death.

"Who the fuck is it!" she yelled as she raised her bedroom window, but a smile quickly appeared on her face when she saw who it was.

"Open up, bitch!" Kamari shouted.

"Oh my God! You get on my nerves." She laughed. "Here I come." She just knew it was Kane coming over there to crash out on her.

When Thyri opened the door Kamari had food for them.

"Awe boo, thank you! I swear you're the fuckin' shit!" Thyri told her as she grabbed her for a hug. "You always know when I'm hungry, with my greedy ass."

"Come on, you know I got you. What the hell was you about to do?" Kamari quizzed when she peeped Thyri in a bra and booty shorts. "Don't tell me that damn nigga is upstairs."

Thyri couldn't do anything but laugh at her friend because that was the typical move for her, and she knew Kamari didn't have faith that she was done with Kane once and for all.

"No girl. Kane isn't upstairs. I was about to get in the shower. I told you this time I'm going to stand on big business because

I'm going to court on him. Shit, they need to hurry up though. I don't want this to be prolonged at all," she explained. "I know my word doesn't mean a lot these days, but just watch."

"Oh, damn. Now I feel bad for not giving you the benefit of the doubt, boo," Kamari admitted.

"It's okay, girl. I understand. I really do, but what you bring my greedy ass to eat?" Thyri asked, changing the subject.

"You know all my ass eat is Chinese food." She giggled. "I swear they got crack in this shit because they got me hooked."

"Oh lord. I'm cool with anything free," Thyri replied jokingly. "You know I got paid yesterday, so I'm about to head up to Rainbow Nails on Bessemer."

"Shit, why you ain't call me? I wanna go too." Kamari pulled the food from the bags and put everything on the coffee table.

"Um, because ya ass ain't give me time, heffa. I was going to get my shower and eat first, but you showed up right on time," Thyri told her.

"Oh, okay, 'cause I was about to say. I didn't want to have to kick ya ass," Kamari told her, slapping her arm. "Since the shackles are off now, let's go out tonight."

"Girl, I'm not trying to go out and run into Kane. He's annoying as fuck, and this time I'm going to be the one going to jail," Thyri told her as she munched down on a crab rangoon.

"Girl, fuck that boy! Trust me, he doesn't want no smoke, and I'm sure he ain't that damn stupid. Kane knows his ass will be locked up for even being around you. So come on, let's go. Please, Thyri. It's been too long since we hit the club, and who knows, we might find some fine ass niggas up in there to kick it with," Kamari pleaded.

Thyri rolled her eyes because clubbing was never her thing, but she needed other human interactions as well if she truly wanted to rid her life of Kane. She sighed heavily and reluctantly agreed to go.

"I'll go but I'm bringing my strap with me," she informed her friend. "If that nigga tries anything that will be his last time."

"Cool, but you know you can't take that shit in the club girl, so it has to stay in the car, friend."

"Yeah, I know and that's fine, so it can stay in the car, but I'm giving you fair warning. If Kane's ass comes up there on bullshit, I'm catching a case!"

"Calm down, killa." Kamari laughed. "We gone be good."

"Oh, I know we are! And that's on what? Mary had a little lamb," Thyri told her, and they laughed in unison.

After they ate, Thyri took her shower and they headed to the nail salon...

LATER THAT NIGHT...

"Girl, hurry the hell up! I'm not trying to go all late. It's ladies' night and that free entry and them two-dollar Apple Crown shots sound good as hell," Kamari rushed.

"I'm coming now," Thyri replied as she added the finishing touches to her look for the night. She wore an all-red maxi dress with some black heels that laced up her legs.

Thyri stood 5'5" tall, and her body was well proportioned with big DD-cup titties and a fat ass, thick and curvy in all the right places. Her hips were to die for. She's a light caramel complexion with freckles. Her body is covered with various tattoos and piercings. Her looks matched her personality. She was just as beautiful on the outside as she was on the inside.

Kamari had a good buzz going on and knew it was time for them to hurry up because if not, she would be too drunk to drive. Kamari was on her social media trying to keep from drinking so much of the Hennessey. Her face lit up when she saw messages from her ex, Jay, begging to be back with her.

I know I hurt you and it was never my intention, Kamari. I prayed so hard for a woman like you and when I got you, I fumbled you. I don't like to be the way that I am. I just hope that one day you can forgive me, please. Remember that I loved you very much. I should have told you, but I was too afraid to lose you.

Kamari got disgusted all over again. She had forgiven him for burning her but hearing from him nearly a year later took her back to the day she went to the clinic thinking she was pregnant. The way he had treated her was gut-wrenching, and the pain came rushing back too fast.

Thank you for reaching out and apologizing, but it took a damn year. It's whatever, just leave me alone. Don't worry, I been forgave you, I'm just in a better place with my life. I wish you the best, she replied, blocking him.

"Damn girl, why you mean mugging like that?" Thyri asked as she walked into the living room.

"You not gonna believe who just hit me up, girl."

"Oh shit, who?" Thyri asked, intrigued.

"Muthafuckin' Jay! He called himself apologizing or whatever. I kindly thanked his ass and blocked him before he could reply. You know I'm petty as hell, so I waited until I saw the three dots." She busted out laughing. In a way, Kamari was happy to hear from Jay. That man had her heart in a chokehold for at least two years.

"Bitch! No he didn't! What the hell was he thinking? Like you were about to give his weird ass another shot. His ass should have apologized when that shit happened."

"Girl, I'm so over that nigga. That's why we're going out tonight, to catch some new ones," Kamari replied, holding her hand in the air to give Thyri a high five.

"Aht, aht, whore. The last thing I want to do is find another problem. However, I might find my next sneaky link," she replied.

"Yeah, exactly bitch, so cut the bullshit."

"Whatever, I'm ready. Let's go so I can get back and get into my big ass bed," Thyri told her.

"It's about damn time, girl. It took you long enough. You look good as fuck, boo! I hope Kane do see how you poppin' out."

"Hell nah, I'm good. Your ass is driving too. I'm just getting my L's back from that DUI I got in 2021."

"Ugh, friend, come on. I'll fill your tank up if you drive," Kamari pleaded. "You know my Maxima is raggedy."

"Negative boo, you can drive my car if you want to, but I'm not driving," she told her.

"You annoy me so much," she replied, taking Thyri's keys as they headed out.

By the time they made it to the club, there was a long ass line wrapped around the building.

"Hell no, I'm good on this. Let's go to a bar or something," Thyri complained.

"Absolutely not, these outfits are too good to be sitting at the damn bar, friend."

Thyri just knew this was a sign that she shouldn't even go into the club. For all she knew Kane would be there all up in her face pissing her off and ruining her night like he usually did.

By the time they finally made it inside, the blunt they had smoked outside kicked in hard as hell. They were both fucked up.

Thyri's vibe was fucked up soon as she saw Kane and someone who looked to be his new punching bag heading up to the VIP. *Better her than me,* she thought.

"Bitch, I'm ready to go," she complained.

"Hell no, what's wrong with you?" Kamari huffed as they headed to the bar for another round of drinks.

"So, you didn't just see Kane and that bitch walk up in here?" Thyri huffed. "I don't got time for his bullshit, girl. I already know if he sees me shit about to go left."

"Fuck no! Where he at?" she said, looking around trying to spot him.

"I guess he still over there by the door," Thyri replied, not wanting to make eye contact with him trying to point him out.

"Oh shit, is that his new girl?" Kamari asked, excited.

"Bitch, I hope so. Maybe then he'll leave me alone. Let her get her ass beat a few times and I bet she will be gone too. That nigga gotta be gay as angry as he is with women."

"Good, because we not about to let him fuck our night up!"

she shouted over the music. "Come on, let's fuck this dance floor up."

Thyri slammed her double shot and headed to the dance floor. Not even twenty minutes later, Kane was being escorted out of the club because he had choked the girl up that he was with.

Thank God that fool ain't see me, Thyri thought. She continued to enjoy her night Kane free. Once he left, she was able to really let her hair down and enjoy herself...

CHAPTER THREE

The next morning Thyri woke up from her slumber with her head knocking. She looked around and realized that she was in a hotel room. She turned around and faced Lamar, a guy that she had crept with on occasion when she and Kane were breaking up every five minutes.

Thyri, what the hell were you thinking? she thought. She looked on the floor and saw her dress. As she tried to ease out of the bed Lamar woke up.

"Where are you going, girl? I got the room for two nights," he spoke, pulling her by the waist closer to him.

"Aww, damn love, I got to cover a shift today. I got to be there in the next two hours so I gotta get going," she lied. She couldn't believe that she even took it there with him again. He was cool and ate pussy like he was getting paid to do so, but he wasn't for her.

"Damn boo," he huffed, sitting up and kissing her on the cheek.

"It's all good. Maybe we can pick this up another day when I don't have to work." She proceeded to get dressed so she could get out of there as quick as possible.

"Shit," she huffed.

"What's up, bae?"

Thyri looked at him with a tight grin and a crazy look on her face. *He must still be drunk saying that shit,* she thought.

"It's nothing. I just forgot that I didn't drive last night, but it's cool. I'll just order a rideshare. Go back to sleep," she replied, opening the door.

"Cut that shit out, girl. I got you! What kind of man would I be to let you just wait for a rideshare when I got a whip?" he told her, getting up out the bed. "Just give me five minutes."

Thyri took that time to check her phone. She pulled it from her bag and noticed that she had seven missed calls from a blocked number. She already knew who it was, so she didn't bother listening to the voicemails. She went straight to the half dozen texts that Kamari had sent. Before she could reply Lamar was walking out the bathroom ready to go.

"Come on girl, let's make this shit shake," he spoke. "I wish you would call out today and let me make up that missed money for ya fine ass."

Thyri rolled her eyes and lied to him again. "I wish I could boo, but I can't miss or be late for work for the next thirty days. They got me on probation for missing too many days."

"Damn. It's cool though, I ain't going nowhere," he told her, slapping her ass so hard that she wanted to turn around and slap him across the face.

The entire car ride was quiet and awkward as hell. Thyri didn't know what to say because she knew she wouldn't have even entertained him if she wasn't drunk the night before. Her mind went straight to Kamari. She knew her girl was going to clown her ass to no end soon as she talked to her.

The second they got to the intersection on 16th Street and Summit Ave at the stop light, someone smashed into the back of his SUV causing Thyri to scream and duck because she didn't know what was going on. Her heart raced and her body shook uncontrollably. She thought she was about to release her bowels all over the front seat.

"Oh, fuck naw!" he barked, hopping out his ride to check whoever had just hit his truck. He was quickly met with several blows to his head and face. It came so fast that he didn't know who was even doing it.

"What the fuck!" she snapped, turning around to see who was behind the assault when she heard Lamar yelling.

"Shut the fuck up and get out the damn car!" Kane instructed. Just that quick he'd beat Lamar to a bloody pulp.

"Nigga, are you insane? You have lost your motherfuckin' mind!" she looked over at Lamar as he tried several times to get off the ground to no avail.

Thyri nearly passed out when she saw all the blood pouring from his face. She knew this nigga was thrown but not so much that he would nut the fuck up enough to try and kill someone in broad daylight. She knew someone had to see what had just happened, so she waited to hear sirens. That way she would be rid of this cancer for the rest of her life. She wasn't that lucky though. Thyri just knew that he was over her since he had a new victim.

Kane sped off so fast they almost crashed into Cook-Out. Thyri was livid and hurt at the same time. She wasn't on Lamar like that, but him getting beat up was the last thing she expected to witness. The only thing she thought about was how would she ever be able to apologize to him. Not able to wrap her mind around what had happened, she just sat in silence as tears rolled down her cheeks.

Neither of them said anything until they got to The Highland Hotel in High Point.

"Get the fuck in there," Kane said, shoving her into the room with force. She wanted to fight him but she had no strength left. Her body was weakened by what she'd just witnessed. True enough, she was aware of how Kane had always acted behind her, but this was a new low.

Thyri stood in the corner of the room still visibly shaken up with dried-up tears on her cheeks.

"Why are you acting like I'm holding you hostage, girl? Go get in the shower and clean yourself up," he ordered, tossing her a shirt and some shorts.

Maybe this fucker doesn't know the definition of kidnapping. Ain't no way he believes this is okay, she thought.

"Are you out of your fuckin' mind, Kane?" she gritted in a low whisper.

"You made me do that shit! I done told you so many times that you're mine, Thyri, and I don't share," he spat, standing from the bed. "Now do what I said! I got some drinks and shit too."

She glared at him out the corner of her eye as she made her way to the bathroom. There was no soul behind his eyes. This was a part of Kane she didn't know. Her heart broke because the little bit of love she had left for him had slowly diminished. There was no coming from this in any shape or form.

They were not together at all, so for him to take it there pissed her off to the fullest. Thyri was sick and tired of having to constantly walk on eggshells because of him and his ignorance.

She ran the shower as she got undressed. Thyri took a long look at herself, and she cried like she never had before. Their relationship was toxic to say the least, but she was over it all. She didn't want to wish bad on him, but she prayed that God would remove him from her life. At this point, all she could do was pray.

As the hot water beat off her back like a drum, she drifted to another time, but even that was interrupted with trauma. Tears poured even heavier down her cheeks with every breath she took.

"Aye, come up out of there," Kane demanded, banging on the door and scaring her half to death.

Still lost in her thought,s Thyri closed her eyes and let the water splash all over her face. The only thing that snapped her little trance was when Kane kicked the bathroom door in and snatched the shower curtain back.

Frozen in place, Thyri just looked at him with a cold stare. She had nothing left for the man she once wanted to spend the rest of her life with.

"Shit baby, I thought you tried to leave me or something. Get out so I can suck on that pussy. You really thought that little piece of paper was gone stop me, huh?" he taunted. "I been told you I'm not going anywhere."

This sick motherfucka is beyond mental. I hope he don't think that shit he did got my pussy wet, she thought. Yeah, in the beginning, it was cute when he got jealous behind her, but this was the straw that broke the camel's back. She truly hated this man with a passion.

Thyri quickly complied by following him back to the room. Her emotions were all over the place. She didn't know whether she was coming or going. Praying, counting, taking deep breaths, nothing was calming her spirits at all.

When Kane hit a line of cocaine, that's when it all started making sense. Never in the time that she'd known him did he ever do any other drug than weed. That mixed with drinking and high emotions, Thyri knew she had to go with the flow, at least until she could get away from him...

CHAPTER FOUR

Deion had to practically fight Indya to get out the house.
He knew that she wouldn't be on board with him
leaving her in Charlotte and going to Greensboro, but
she needed to give him a break. The constant arguing was
breaking him in ways he never expected. Gianna was the only
reason he even bothered staying with her to begin with. Indya did
nothing but nag him over anything and it was tiresome. If he
didn't answer her calls or texts, she would track his location and
pull up to wherever he was. He figured if he got this break then
they could possibly save what was left of their relationship. If not,
he was prepared to move his business to Greensboro. Ever since
COVID, business hadn't been the same.

Before taking his trip, he turned off the location on his phone
because there was no way in hell he was going to have her popping
up on him in Greensboro.

"What's up? You been out here for a few days and been stuck
up in this house," his homeboy Legend said to him.

"Shit, you know I only came out here for one thing, and
that's to make a little bit of bread and get some much-needed
time away from Indya. She has been down my back every fuckin'
hour, blowing my phone up. The last thing I wanted to do is

upset her further, but I had to get the hell away," Deion admitted.

"You know it's all love out this way. Shit, we can make a little bit of money and I'll take you to a few spots that I'm sure you will enjoy. Shit, I love my city. I'm just mad you ain't been out here in so long."

"Man, the past few years have been hell. Besides working and fighting with Indya, I haven't had much downtime."

"Nigga, ya ass be finding the time to cheat or your shorty wouldn't be at you like that," he said laughing. "I'm just fuckin' with you G, but on the real, be careful with that. Indya seems like she doesn't play that shit."

"I know you not talking, nigga! You been a playa since grade school," he replied.

"You know it, my boy," Legend said, pointing his finger at Deion.

"I'm telling you, watch how this shit move when we hit the club. You gone fuck around and never go back home! Feel me?" Legend explained.

"I'm all in, for sure. Shit, I didn't have no plans on clubbing but fuck it, you only live once."

Legend was a tall, light-skin, burly-looking brother that didn't take no shit. He minded his business and stayed out the way but if someone fucked with anyone he rocked with, they would be dealt with accordingly.

"Nah, on some real shit. I wish Indya was up for moving back out this way, but she stuck on the money she makes at the firm in Charlotte. I like that shit but ain't nothing like the Boro. This will forever be home, man."

"You need to talk to her, man. We could run the city," Legend replied as his doorbell rang. "Shit, that's probably Philly."

Deion let the thought ponder for a few seconds but let it diminish because that wasn't him anymore, but if the real estate market didn't get right soon, he might take Legend up on his offer.

When Legend bent the corner, he sighed heavily. It wasn't Philly but his baby mother Casha. He knew she was coming over to get on his nerves. Their relationship was that of a bitter breakup. They loved one another but they couldn't get along to save their lives. Of course, they still messed around when they shouldn't have been because Casha didn't know her place.

"Fuck!" he cursed.

Although she saw him heading to the door, she kept ringing the doorbell like a lunatic. "Hurry up, nigga!" she yelled, looking through the window.

"Got damn, why the hell are you hitting my shit like that?" he barked as he snatched the door open.

"Why the fuck have you been ignoring my calls, Legend!?" she yelled, pushing her way inside.

"Man, don't come up in here on all that, Casha. I been fuckin' busy!" he barked, heading back to the game room.

"Hey, what's up, Casha," Deion spoke.

She turned to him and rolled her eyes. "Whatever."

"Nah, don't come up in here with all that rude shit, Casha. Speak like you got some sense or you can get the hell out," Legend told her.

"It's cool G, I understand," Deion replied and went to the other side of the room and made himself a drink.

"Sup," she replied. "Anyway, back to the reason I'm here. Who you fuckin', Legend? We both know the only time you get on this funny shit is when you talking to a new bitch! So, where the fuck she at?"

"Man, I ain't about to talk about nothing with you. Where the twins? You broke your neck coming here but didn't bring my kids. Who I'm laying this pipe to is not your concern!"

Deion just sat back and laughed at them. This took him right back to his home. He didn't miss those petty arguments that he and Indya had, but somehow it kind of made him feel right at home. He poured up a few shots for him and Legend. He would have asked Casha if she wanted one but by the way she was acting, a drink was the last thing she needed.

Casha was a true stallion. She was 5' 11" with big ass titties, a perfect apple-shaped ass, and the curves to make any man get caught in her beauty. However, the attitude she had took away from that.

"They at my momma's house, nigga! Where else would they be? I know you got some bitches in here," she huffed, looking around.

"Go on with all of that! Why the fuck you ain't bring them with you? This why we always into it because you still think I'm your man! Take ya ass home!" he barked as he started playing pool. Legend was so fed up with her and the constant drama that followed her. She was cool unless he missed a call, because she assumed that he was laid up with the next female. Most times she would be right, but who was she to try and control the situation? Legend was far from stupid. He knew that Casha did her own thing, but he couldn't care less. That was the difference between them because she cared mostly when whoever she was fucking was unavailable.

"I don't know why you insist on playing with me, nigga. You know I'm gone smack your shit every time!" Deion told him.

"Put ya money where ya mouth is then," Legend barked.

It didn't matter what it was, Deion couldn't help himself when it came to gambling. You would think he had enough by now, but the urge came like an addiction he couldn't control.

"So, you just gone act like I'm not right here?" Casha grilled. "Look, I need some money. The girls need some shoes, and they start daycare next week."

"Damn, so you came here for money, huh? I should have known that shit!"

"Yup, I sure did, and to see why you keep ignoring my calls. I know you fuckin' somebody! When I find out who, it's up!" she warned.

"Man, here," Legend snapped, passing her eleven hundred dollars. "I don't have to answer your calls, girl."

"Nigga, this all you got?" she spat.

"That's all you're getting, now get out my fuckin' house, Casha!" he demanded, dismissing her.

"I swear you get on my damn nerves, Legend. Slanging all that shit and be giving me this bullshit money!"

"Bye Felicia," he replied nonchalantly.

Casha gave him the finger and stormed out the house.

"And I thought my shorty be bugged out," Deion spoke. "I don't think she like me though." He chuckled.

"She doesn't like nobody. That bitch is miserable. I swear I wish I never had kids with her, but I wouldn't trade them for the world."

"Yeah, I feel that."

Deion was happy to be there, but he knew he had to get Indya out the way for a while, or she would be trying to pull up on him. That wasn't something he needed to be bothered with...

CHAPTER FIVE

"I have been here for a damn hour! When can I talk to someone?" Kamari huffed as she paced the floor at the police station.

"It'll be just a few more minutes, ma'am," the receptionist replied, smacking on her gum.

"Yeah, you keep saying that lady, but my friend is missing! Ugh, I swear to fuckin' God!" she huffed, walking off. Her nerves were a wreck.

She had been calling and texting Thyri all morning and got no reply or anything. She even tried to call Lamar via his social media but still came up empty. The only other thing she knew to do was to go file a missing person's report, because for as long as she and Thyri had been friends, she'd never not reached out. Her soul told her something was wrong.

"Yes ma'am, you can come with me," a tall Black officer spoke. "I'm Officer Shepard and I'll be taking your report."

"Thank you. It's about time. I've been waiting over an hour," she huffed and rolled her eyes at the rude woman at the front desk.

She followed him into his office, her anxiety riding shotgun.

"Have a seat," he told her, closing the door.

"I know it hasn't been forty-eight hours, but I know something is wrong."

"Okay, tell me why you think your friend is missing," he replied nonchalantly.

"We went out last night and she left with one of her guy friends. I've tried calling them and I can't get a reply," she anxiously answered.

"Your friend is a grown woman. Is it possible that she just doesn't want to be found?" he quizzed.

"No, she wouldn't do that. When I say we're best friends, that's what I mean. We are practically glued to the hip, Officer Shepard. I'm telling you, something is wrong," she insisted.

"Okay, I hear you, ma'am."

"No, you don't! Y'all motherfuckas don't ever want to do shit when it comes to black or brown people missing. Y'all never take that shit serious!" she barked, standing up hastily. "I can name at least four missing black girls from this area right now and I haven't heard nothing about it!"

"If you haven't noticed, I'm a black man so that statement doesn't make any sense young lady," he replied, offended.

"Nah, you bleed blue, let's not forget," she spat. The last thing Kamari wanted to do was spaz out, but this man was trying the patience she no longer had.

"I'll tell you what. Give me your friend's phone number and her guy friend's name and number. I will try giving them a call. If they don't answer, I'll investigate it for you, but I can't make any promises," he told her, turning his nose up.

The second Kamari gave Officer Shepard Lamar's full name, he stopped writing immediately.

"Lamar Francisco?" he quizzed with a raised brow.

"Yes, but why did you say it like that?" she inquired with a raised brow.

"Listen, I'm not supposed to speak on any open investigations, but ..."

"Oh my God, please don't tell me she's dead! Oh God, what am I gonna do," she cut him off, crying.

"No ma'am. You didn't let me finish. He was the only one in the vehicle."

"What the fuck!" she shouted, standing to her feet. "Is he dead?" Without warning, tears fell from her eyes like thick raindrops hitting pavement.

"So where is Thyri? She was just with him last night. Do you think he did something to her? Oh my God!"

Kamari felt like she was about to lose her mind. She was so afraid that her friend was lying somewhere dead or badly injured and she couldn't do anything about it. She wondered why Thyri wasn't in the car with Lamar. Why she hadn't tried to call her. Kamari's mind was racing a million miles a second.

"Since I know that she was with him, I promise that I am going to investigate. I want you to give me your number so if I come across some new information, I'll let you know. I'm also going to give you my business card so you can call me if you need to," he told her.

"Okay, thank you so much. Please keep me informed," she replied, still shaking and trying to dry her tears.

As soon as she left, she went straight to Thyri's apartment. She was hoping she had made it home by then, but she wasn't so lucky. Kamari even asked a few neighbors that were standing outside if they had seen her.

"No, I haven't seen her since yesterday," an older lady spoke up.

"Okay, thank you. Can I give you my number so you can call me when or if you see her, please?"

"Yes baby, no problem," she replied.

Kamari gave her number to the woman and left. She didn't know what else to do but go home and pray she'd hear from her friend sooner than later...

Thyri lay in the bed beside Kane while he slept. Her heart raced with anticipation and fear, but she knew that if she was going to live through his mental break, she would have to either do something drastic or suffer through whatever he was about to do to her, and she wasn't ready by far to meet her maker.

Knowing that Kane was high and drunk as hell, she knew that it was now or never.

Her heart rate increased as she eased out the pissy-smelling hotel bed. Thyri knew that he was a light sleeper and being inebriated didn't matter. On a good night he could hear her creep off to the bathroom. Thyri knew that if she stayed, she would possibly end up like Lamar, fucked up and hoping for help.

The only way she could escape would be through the front door because there were no other ways out. She didn't have her phone because he'd broken it and thrown it out on their way to High Point. Shortly after, he sent several blows to her face, knocking her beneath him.

Thyri was so scared her body shook without warning. Her palms were sweaty, and she thought her bowels would expel all over the place at any moment.

Never in her whole life had she ever felt like this. She was scared to stay and too scared to leave in fear of him catching her and possibly ending her life. She knew that he loved her, but the way he'd been acting lately had her feeling like none of what they had been through was worth it. They had been through a lot over the last nine years, but this was bad.

Father God, please give me the strength to get up and leave from this man's side. Cover me in the blood and keep me safe. I want to live. I choose life, just please help me get away from this man for good, she thought, pleading with God.

Although Thyri lost all hope and faith in God when she was younger, she needed to believe that he was there for her at that moment. He was all she had and the only one she could count on to get her free of this situation.

Kane was surprisingly knocked out after all the coke he'd

done. His snoring was consistent and steady, so she took a pillow and placed it in his arms, hoping it would take her place. She also made sure she put another one down by his legs.

As she eased out the bed, people walked by the door talking loudly. She stood frozen in her tracks, trying to hold her pee. Sighing heavily, she closed her eyes tightly and took deep breaths, hoping he wouldn't hear. Lucky for her, he didn't hear a word. His snores didn't miss a beat.

After breathing a sigh of relief, she continued her journey to the door at a steady pace but not moving too slow or fast. When she reached the door, she slowly unlocked both locks while simultaneously looking at Kane. She grabbed her purse and closed her eyes.

Taking several deep breaths, she turned the doorknob while making sure to hold onto it tightly so that it wouldn't make any noise. When she got it open enough to squeeze through, it started squeaking. Kane took a deep breath and changed his position but thankfully, he didn't wake up.

Thyri eased her way through the door. She saw several people standing around but they looked like junkies, so she ignored them and continued her journey. The night air gave her chills, but this was a step in the right direction. She made sure not to shut the hotel door all the way. The last thing she needed was for him to wake up. Making her way to the back of the hotel, she looked around trying to find the perfect escape route.

"Come on girl, you got this," Thyri told herself.

Shortly after, she heard Kane crazily calling her name and was terrified, but she held it together enough to run to a nearby neighborhood. She figured the first place he would look for her would be at a well-lit location like a store, so she made sure to avoid that.

She went to the very first house she saw but there was no answer when she knocked, so she continued her mission. After the third house, a car came speeding down the street. Thyri was uncertain if it was Kane, but she hid behind their bushes just in case it was him. She creeped over to the following house and knocked. Thankfully, an elderly lady came to the door.

"Can I help you dear?"

"Yes ma'am, I'm sorry to bother you, but do you happen to have a phone I can use?" she asked, trying not to seem overly anxious or weird. Of course, her first instinct was to freak out, but she needed to be quick on her feet. Panicking wasn't going to save her.

"How do I know you're not a crazy woman?" she replied, innocently looking behind her.

"I promise you that I am not. My ex-boyfriend just beat me up. I just need to call a ride to come and get me. Please, I'll make my call and be on my way."

Thyri was doing her best to be as sincere as she could because the last thing she wanted to do was to spook the lady.

"Come in, baby," she told Thyri, widening the door.

While looking over her shoulder, Thyri went inside as she was instructed. She stood in the corner by the door and waited for the old lady as she disappeared into another room. She had to pee badly, but she was going to hold it because she didn't want to be a burden to this stranger.

Soon as the lady came back holding onto the cordless phone, her anxiety eased up a little bit.

"Thank you so much," she softly spoke.

"Not a problem," the lady replied with a shaky voice.

Thyri didn't waste no time calling Kamari's line.

"Hello," she answered.

"Come get me," she said, busting out crying, no longer able to hold it back.

"Oh my God! Thyri! Where are you? My God, I've been so worried. I done went to try and file a missing person's report and everything! Are you okay?"

"I don't know. I'm somewhere in High Point." She quickly asked the lady for her address and gave it to Kamari.

"What the fuck happened? Never mind, I'm on the way. Stay

right there," she said, disconnecting the call and not giving Thyri a chance to reply.

Soon as Thyri passed the phone back someone started ringing the doorbell. Thyri nearly dropped to the floor as her limbs became weakened. She just knew this would be her last day on earth.

"Oh my God. Where is your back door?"

"Oh, it's okay sweetheart. That's probably the pie I ordered just before you got here," the lady told her getting up. It was indeed her pizza.

Thyri just wanted to bundle up and cry like a baby. She hated how scared she was of Kane. At one point in time, he was her everything.

"I'm sorry, can I please use your bathroom?" Thyri asked, no longer able to hold her bladder.

"Straight to the back and the first door on the left, honey," she replied, shutting and locking her door and setting the alarm. Erma didn't mind helping, but she wanted to make sure that Thyri's boyfriend didn't come in her home either.

Moments later, Thyri came back and stood over by the door. She was not trying to be a bother to the lady. While in the bathroom she was finally able to see the damage Kane had done. Her heart ached but sadly, it was nothing new to her. She was surprised that after all the beatings he'd given her she didn't have brain damage.

"Thank you," she said, attempting to leave.

"Have a seat and grab a slice, young lady," Erma urged.

"Thank you, but I'm alright," she politely replied.

"I won't hear of it. I'm certain your ride won't be here within the next five minutes. It's okay, you're safe."

Reluctantly, Thyri sat down on the edge of the chair and ate a slice of pizza. Even though the lady was nice to her she was still very much uncomfortable.

"I am so sorry. My name is Thyri. What is your name?" she asked.

"My name is Erma, honey. It's an unfortunate situation that you're in right now, but it's a pleasure meeting you."

They talked for another twenty or so minutes before Kamari showed up. She raced to the door, praying Thyri was still there waiting.

Erma greeted her and invited her inside as well. Kamari followed behind her and couldn't contain her excitement when she saw Thyri.

"Oh my God, I have been looking for you girl. What happened with Lamar?" she said all in one breath.

"Awe, thank you for being concerned, babe. Ms. Erma, this is my best friend Kamari," Thyri said, introducing them. She didn't want to go into specifics while there. Kamari could wait for the tea.

"Hello, honey," she spoke.

"Yes ma'am, nice to meet you and thank you for taking care of my friend," Kamari told her.

"It wasn't a problem. I don't get out much, so this has been a treat for me," she honestly spoke. "You can take a load off."

"I'm going to get out your hair. Again, I can't thank you enough for what you did for me, Ms. Erma," Thyri told her. Erma was a beautiful lady. She looked to be in her seventies with gray hair.

"Hush it up. It was a pleasure. Now you girls be safe," she replied as she walked them to the door.

Once Thyri got into her friend's car, she felt safer than she had in a while.

"I'm not going home. I don't know if Kane will try to come over there and I don't want to ever see his ass. That nigga done lost his shit. I don't know what he's going through, but I don't want to be a part of whatever it is, girl."

"So, you know you must fill me in on the details. You can just come to my crib, boo."

"Nah, that ain't about to happen either. I need to get a room until that psychopath is locked up or something. You just don't understand, Kamari. He's nothing like he used to be."

"So, you been with him this whole time?"

"Yeah, bitch, after he drug me out of Lamar's truck! He beat the shit out of him, and I didn't have a choice in the matter. What's so cold is he acted like nothing had happened when we got to the hotel. He was nonchalant as fuck!"

"Yo, that nigga is unhinged! What the fuck! Okay, so we can stop by Walmart and grab a few toiletries and I'm coming with you because you don't need to be alone," Kamari told her. "I want to lay hands on that fool. He's always messing your face up."

"No, I don't want you in my shit, girl. You'll be safer away from me," she said through tears.

"Nah, I don't care what you say, Thyri. I'm not leaving you alone until he is locked up. Fuck that!"

"Bet, I'm about to make a quick little pickup order. I'll grab us something to sleep in too."

Kamari didn't expect Thyri to tell her that Kane was behind the madness, but she wasn't that much surprised either. He was just ignorant and dangerous like that. She was just glad that her friend escaped with only a black eye and busted lip, but her heart broke into pieces when Thyri told her how he had forced himself on her...

CHAPTER SIX

"Aye, I was thinking that we can hit the strip club on Gate City Blvd instead of the regular shit," Legend spoke.

"Nigga, you just be changing plans while we are riding. I swear you're still that same annoying, indecisive little boy I grew up with," Deion clowned.

"Cut it out. Are you down or not? And little boy? I'm a grown ass man, my boy," Legend replied.

"Fuck it, might as well enjoy my night since you got me to come out in the first place," he huffed.

"Shit nigga, you can't be out here cooped up in the crib every day and night. Here," he said, passing him the blunt. "You got to get out and enjoy yourself while you're here."

"Yeah, I do need to relax and not be so damn uptight."

"That's all I'm saying, bruh. You wanna hit this bottle?" Legend asked.

"You should already know the vibes," Deion replied. "Pass that shit."

"Got damn! This shit is lit early as hell! I know we about to make some good ass money up in here," Legend said, passing Deion the Henny.

After Deion took a few swigs and hit the blunt again, they

headed inside. The line to get inside was wrapped around the building but Legend was able to get them straight inside.

"I see you, my nigga! You got it like that!" Deion said as they walked inside.

"Yeah, that's my little cousin. He stays looking out. I tried to get him to work with me but he wanna stay clean. Shit, that nigga could be big time if he stepped over this way. He has the perfect job for it, man."

Deion's mouth hit the floor when he saw how live it was. He'd been to several strip clubs in Charlotte, but the vibe wasn't anything like this. The Treasure Club had him ready to risk it all. He followed Legend to VIP where they posted up and waited on Philly and a couple of more friends.

Not even an hour later Deion was lit, throwing all kinds of money. He was glad that they stopped at the ATM before they got there. It was all kind of big booty freaks all over him throwing nothing but ass. There was one that caught his eye though.

Tasty was her name, and she was wearing a red lace-front wig and was fine as hell. He knew he must have spent at least three racks on her because he kept getting lap dances.

"Don't hurt yourself, nigga!" Legend yelled over the music, laughing.

"I got this shit," he slurred. "Shorty is like that!"

Soon as the club lights came on, he made sure to get her number. The last thing on his mind was to cheat on his girl, but Tasty was about to get all that stress dick.

Deion was still talking to her when a short light-skinned nigga approached them with a scowl on his face.

"Go get your shit!" he barked, snatching her by the arm.

"Why do you always come in here acting like this, Justin! This is my fuckin' job!" she huffed.

"You good, shorty?" Deion grilled, stepping closer to her.

"Who the fuck is this dusty ass nigga?" he barked. "I suggest you mind your business!" Justin barked.

"Dusty! Nigga, I will end you right here!" Deion barked.

Normally he wouldn't have involved himself in anyone's business, but this dude was being disrespectful.

"Aye, chill out my boy, you don't want this problem," Legend said, stepping in between them.

"Man, fuck you too!" As soon as the words left his mouth, Justin regretted it. Legend's boys Rocky and Philly walked over to them.

"What was that?" Rocky barked. "You already know what time it is, Justin. Don't get fucked up!"

"Can y'all not pull this ghetto shit!" Tasty spat, walking off. "You get on my fuckin' nerves."

"It's cool, I don't want no problems," Justin said, holding his hands in the air. He'd only crossed paths with Rocky one other time and got his ass handed to him. "My bad."

"That shit was crazy, man," Legend said on their way out the club.

When they got in the car, Deion got a call from a private number. He knew it was Indya because he blocked her number before going out. Deion was faded and didn't feel like arguing.

"That nigga ain't want this shit," he slurred.

"Your ass ain't in the position to fight shit," Legend replied, laughing.

"Shit, don't underestimate me, nigga," he said, leaning all the way back in his seat. "I don't think your boy Rocky fuckin' with me."

"Man, trust me, he's cool. It just takes him a minute to feel people out. You saw how he was right there when that nigga tried jumping bad."

"He did that because of you. Not me, my boy, but it doesn't matter for real. I won't be here too much longer."

"Just chill, that's my boy, so if I fuck with you, he does too," Legend replied, pulling off.

"I hear you. Fuck!"

"What's up? You good?" Legend quizzed.

"Yeah, I'm straight. It's my BM blowing me up. I swear that

girl got ESP or something. She knows when I'm having a good time and I swear she tries to fuck it up!"

"Shit, don't answer the phone. I damn sure ignore Casha's ass when she's annoying me, which is daily."

"Man, I have to, she got my daughter," he replied, sitting straight up in his seat. She had blown his buzz.

"Yo?" he answered.

"Wow, is that how we're answering the phone now Deion?!"

"Is Gianna, okay?" he quizzed.

"You're really a class act, Deion. I called to check on you and this is what you do? You're acting like I did something to you," she huffed. "Meanwhile, your dick is sliding up in everything with a hole!"

"I'm good. You just caught me off guard," he lied, ignoring her last comment.

As they drove to the other side of town, Legend hit Casha and told her to meet him at the crib.

"When are you coming back home? It's lonely without you."

Deion silently sighed before answering her. "I'll be back soon enough. Why don't you take this time to spend time with your mom and sister?"

"You and Gianna are the only people I need to worry about. I don't want to fight anymore, baby. We been through too much to just give up." By the way Deion was talking, Indya could tell that he was ready to give up, but she wasn't about to let him do that no matter how he felt.

"Yeah, I know, but look, I need to run. I'll hit you up when I get to the crib," he replied. Deion was willing to tell her whatever to get her off his nerves. He couldn't do shit with her down his back every five minutes.

"Wow! You must have been at the club or some shit! You really are a dick head, Deion! How the fuck are you out there having the time of your life without us?"

"I'll call you back, damn!" he told her, disconnecting the call before she had a chance to reply.

Chapter Seven

Thyri was doing her best to put the day Kane had left sketched in her memory forever behind her to no avail. She was still paranoid that he was going to bust up in her house and kill her. The nightmares didn't help either. Each time she had one, she would get on the phone and call the jail just to make sure he was still there. Of course, they would have to notify her of his release, but she wasn't taking any chances. It didn't matter how much she drank and smoked, the thoughts never diminished.

Kane went back to the hotel that night, so she was able to give Officer Shepard the details of where he was. Being cocky, he didn't think she would turn him in to the police, but that stunt he had pulled was her last straw. He needed to go down for that mess. The whole time they had been together she'd never held him accountable, but those days were over. It was time that she stopped allowing him to live rent free in her head. She was lucky that he wasn't given a bond just yet, because she was sure that his dumb ass mother would get him straight out. Thyri checked the jail website daily to make sure he didn't have one.

Thyri buried herself in work, trying to keep her mind off her reality. She didn't even want to go out anymore. Never would she be able to forget that the last time she went out, someone she cared for was beat within inches of their life. Kane had caused so much damage to Lamar that he was unrecognizable. His jaw was broken in two places, and he had a broken eye socket and three broken ribs after Kane was finished with him. Of course, his family blamed her for what had happened, not realizing what she had to go through after the fact. It was mostly his twin sister who was giving her hell, so Thyri just ignored her.

Kamari was working overtime to try and get her friend to go to therapy, but she wasn't budging. She wasn't a therapist in the least, but she watched videos online to try and figure out how to help Thyri. Anything that she could do, she was doing it because she was determined not to let Kane ruin her friend's life any further. She hated that Thyri gave him so much power over her life even while being in jail.

Thyri felt the need to reach out to Ms. Erma, but she was nervous. This lady had given her so much comfort in her time of need. It was only right that she reached out to her.

Thyri sat up in her bed and sighed heavily. She sparked a cigarette and grabbed the leftover Hennessey that she had sitting beside her bed. She needed herself a stiff drink. It didn't matter that it was nine in the morning, pregaming before starting her day was how she was living these days.

Grabbing her phone and calling Kamari, Thyri hoped she had some good news because she needed to hear it even if it wasn't her good news. The depression was starting to get the best of her, and she was over it all.

"Hey bookie," she answered.

"You sound chipper this morning. What are you doing up so early?"

"Girl, I was about to come over to your crib and bring you some breakfast but since you called, I guess it's not a surprise anymore," she replied.

"Good, because I want to go see that lady that helped me. It's weighing heavy on my heart, and I have to let her know how much I appreciate her. She didn't have to help me, but she did. You don't come across good people like that. I'm about to make a Walmart delivery order and make her a nice basket. You know, with old lady treats." She giggled.

"See, that's why you're so special, Thyri. That is the sweetest thing I've ever heard. I'm not gone lie. I'm always worried about you, but this is a step in the right direction, and I know this will make her day," Kamari spoke honestly. "You need anything else before I come?"

"Yeah, stop by the ABC store and grab a bottle of D'USSÉ boo," she replied confidently.

"Okay, but Thyri, I'm worried about you. I don't like how you been drinking lately. I know you're going through a lot of emotions babe, but I don't want this to fuck you up in the long run."

"I love you dearly Kamari, but let me have this. If anything will fuck me up in the long run, it will be the demons Kane's ass left me with. I didn't want to tell you, but I had to block the jail calls, girl. Now he keeps having different bitches call my phone three-way and shit! Why won't he just leave me alone?"

"Oh, hell naw! You need to figure out how to make him get in trouble. That's ridiculous. You still have an active restraining order, bitch!"

"No shit, Kamari, but trust me, I have tried to figure this out. But if he isn't the one calling me directly, I can't prove it's him."

"That crazy as hell! Kane needs to seek mental health counseling or something."

"Tell me about it," Thyri replied.

"Anyway, I'll be there shortly. Love you," she replied.

"Love you too."

Kamari wanted so badly to fight her on her thought process, but no matter how close they were she would never know exactly what Thyri was going through and for that, she gave her friend grace. She was just going to be there for her friend along the way no matter what she went through.

Thyri couldn't tell her friend that she didn't check into anything. She knew Kamari wouldn't let her live it down. She was thrilled that Kane was no longer in her way, but she also still felt bad for him in some sick twisted way.

By the time Kamari got there Thyri was feeling herself, singing along to some old-school jams.

"Heyyy, my baby," she said as she opened the door for Kamari. *'Still, nobody want a nigga havin' shit! If I ruled the world and everything in it, sky's the limit I push the Q-45 Infiniti,'* she sang along with Nas. She loved that man like he was her husband. It didn't matter how old the song was, she blasted it anyway.

"Hey boo, I see ya ass is feeling it," she said jokingly. "I'm trying to be on what you on."

"You know it," Thyri said, embracing her in a tight hug. "I don't know where I'd be without you girl. Thank you for always having my back, loving my crazy ass unconditionally," she said through tears. "What did I do to deserve you girl."

"Aht, aht, don't start that crying shit, boo. You know my ass will break down in a heartbeat. Thyri, I'm lucky to have you."

"Shut up, you know I'm a crybaby," Thyri replied jokingly.

"Shit, depending on the situation, I think we both are for real," Kamari replied, locking the door back.

Kamari put their Bojangles on the ottoman and they dug into their food.

"Are you still having nightmares?" Kamari asked.

"Girl yes, and I swear it doesn't matter what I do they just won't go away. I can't believe that fucker called himself kidnapping me," she replied, laughing.

"I damn sure can, he's mental! You really need to see someone, you probably got PTSD or some shit, girl. Your life was spared because God has a purpose for you here on earth. I know it might not seem like it given what you've been through, but you must find it somewhere in your heart to let him in, boo."

"Girl, we have a love-hate relationship, but God knows my heart, Kamari. I know it doesn't seem like it, but I love him. Yes,

I've had a fucked-up road and maybe I should see someone. I'll think about it since you're not letting this go."

"Thank you. That's all I want. Anyway, I was wondering if you wanted to step out Friday night. Please." Kamari smiled wide, showing her pearly whites. "I love you."

"I honestly don't know. I'm not ready for all that. You know motherfuckas gone be all up in my face asking questions and shit."

"I get it boo, but look, we can go and if you're not feeling it then we can leave," she pleaded. "You need to get out of this house. Going to work doesn't count because it's something you have to do."

"You get on my nerves." Sighing heavily, Thyri reluctantly agreed. Soon as she did, someone rang her doorbell and scared them half to death. It was her Walmart delivery.

Kamari didn't want to seem pushy, she just thought that getting out the house might do Thyri some good.

They chatted while they sipped their drinks and munched on their food. It felt good finally being able to relax without fearing that Kane would come over and try to start a problem with her as he usually did.

"I think I went a little bit overboard," Thyri spoke. "I'm not trying to do too much, you know?"

"Nah, this is cool. Ms. Erma is going to love everything," she responded as they continued pilling the gifts into the brown basket that she had also purchased. Thyri had gotten her some house slippers, a robe, various amounts of candy, two large candles, and a teddy bear that had 'Thank you' across its chest.

Once they were all done, they headed straight downtown and went to the floral shop on S. Greene St. Thyri didn't think her basket was complete without flowers and balloons.

"Lord, you are going to have this lady spoiled," Kamari teased playfully.

"She deserves it, girl. I owe her my life, because only God

knows where I'd be right now if I hadn't dipped out on Kane when I did."

Every time she thought of that day it made her emotional. She really hated everything about her situation. Since Kane didn't have a bond, she prayed that they would give him some real time in jail. It seemed like he had a damn get-out-of-jail-free card every time he was arrested. Thyri was going to keep her fingers crossed that this time would be different...

CHAPTER EIGHT

Deion stared at Tasty shaking her thick ass in his face. His dick grew with every grind she did. He grabbed her by the waist and pulled her closer to his stiffness.

"Damn, I see somebody is feeling me," she teased as she turned around.

"Fuck yeah! You know you like it," he said, licking his juicy lips.

Tasty stared into his eyes as seductively as she could. Her pussy got wet by the way he looked at her. She slowly unzipped his True Religion jeans and got on her knees.

"Is this what you want?" she purred, licking her lips.

"Hell yeah," he whispered, laying back.

When she pulled his dick from his pants, she slowly let it enter her mouth, which was heavily salivated. She sloppily sucked and spat on his dick, sending him into another world. "Fuck," he chanted over and over. Grabbing the back of her lace front, he shoved her mouth further down on his shaft causing her to gag. He was fucking her face with force. He needed to bust a nut something serious.

"Get up," he demanded.

Doing as she was told Tasty eased up off his dick. She licked her lips and smiled at him.

"Bend over," he told her while pulling a condom from his pocket. He put it on and entered her from the back so he could watch her ass bounce while he pounded her guts.

"Aw shit daddy, fuck this pussy," she moaned.

"Yeah, take this dick," he grunted slapping her ass. "Shut the fuck up!" A few more pumps and Deion released.

"Damn shorty, that shit was good."

"Yeah, it was. When we gone make this happen again?" Tasty wasn't exactly interested in anything with Deion but he spent money like it grew on trees and this was just the type of nigga she craved. Someone that could match her fly and drop that cash on her.

"We'll have to see about that shorty," he replied with a wide grin. There was nothing about her that made him want to take it there again. He just needed a nut nothing more.

"Just know that I had fun," she said kissing his cheek.

Once they left the blue room, they parted ways. Deion made his way back to the VIP section they had.

"Damn nigga, I know you was up in there clapping cheeks because y'all was in there too long just for a dance," Legend teased, and his boys laughed.

Deion couldn't do shit but smile, he quickly wiped the wide smile away when he noticed how they all were looking at him.

"Nigga, I hope you strapped ya shit up cause shorty a pass around for sure," Rocky said laughing.

"Shit, I for damn sure ain't running up in no hoe raw," Deion replied. "Fuck outta here what kind of nigga you think I am?" Being offended was an understatement.

"Nah, but on some G shit, I know you needed that shit by the way your girl been buggin'," Legend said laughing. "Maybe ya ass can relax and focus more."

"Y'all niggas got jokes tonight," he replied as he grabbed up on of the bottles they had in their section.

"Shit nigga, I just came out the white room with fine ass Pandora over there," Philly said pointing in the direction of a thick ass chocolate girl on the pole. "These hoes be down for whatever so why the fuck not?"

"Philly, you stay tricking on these hoes," Rocky said, and they all laughed. "You gone fuck around and catch some shit and Marisha gone cut ya dick off if she finds out."

"What they say, it ain't trickin' if you got it so don't be salty nigga," Philly barked. "And I'm sure she be fuckin' off too that bitch ain't innocent."

"Cut that shit out. Y'all niggas both acting like some hoes," Legend spoke.

Deion looked around at the friend group that he'd just entered and was glad to be there.

Across town Thyri waited for her friend to get dressed so they could head out.

"I don't understand why we got to hit up a strip club. I mean I'm always down for seeing them hoes shake some ass, but I thought we were gonna just go to a regular club," she complained.

"Girl, because we need to go where the niggas at and trust me you won't be worried about motherfuckas all in ya grill about that Kane shit," Kamari replied. "They're too busy looking at all the pussy up in there."

"Yeah, you got a point cause ain't none of them niggas finna be checking for me. All they gone have on their mind elsewhere," she said laughing as she threw her shot of DeLeón.

"Shit spark that gas up. This pregame gotta hit because I'm trying to throw this money," Kamari said as she pulled five hundred ones from her handbag.

"Yeah, I'm glad we hit the bank before it closed because I was only bout to have like a hunnid for real."

Kamari is a thick chocolate sister with long beautiful hair that flow down her back. She stands at 5" 7' tall with a homegrown shape. Nothing too crazy but she was petite.

By the time they made it to the club it was jumping.

"Oh, my God, I can't wait to get up in here. Thank you for getting me out the house because honestly, I really needed it. I'm so tired of feeling miserable every day," Thyri honestly spoke.

"Girl, you know I got you forever. Although you won't take ya ass to a therapist or something clubbin' it is," she said as they got out the car.

"Ugh, I just want to have a good night girl it's been too damn long since I was able to let my hair down and really enjoy myself without Kane's ass creeping in the shadows," Thyri told her.

"Oh, we most definitely are boo. Don't you worry."

Walking in the club Thyri felt right at home. She thought she would clam up, but this felt so relaxing. She was glad to get out the decided to go. First thing she did was order a dance and a bottle. The girlies were eating up. She had to give it to them. Some of the finest women in Greensboro graced the stages and gave their best performances.

Thyri was lit singing along with the music like she was about to get up and throw some ass with them. Cardi B and Megan Thee Stallion's latest song was blasting through the speakers.

'*Nigga, eat this ass like a plum (plum)*
This pussy tight like a nun (nun)
Better chew it up like its gum (gum)
Then wipe your mouth when you done (okay)
I'm hot like Nevada, pussy get popped, Piñata
Bitch, I look like money (like money)
You could print my face on a dollar' beat it up!

"Damn bitch, not your ass diving straight in like that!" Kamari teased as she shouted out over the music.

"Hell, yeah bitch! I'm gone have fun no matter what!" she yelled slurring. "You know I love this song boo. I know they had better play 'WAP' too."

They partied and drank throwing money at the dancers until they noticed the fine ass brothas looking at them from a far.

"Girl, you see what I see?" Thyri asked her friend.

"If you're talking about them fine ass niggas over in the VIP section gawking over here at us then hell yeah, I sure the fuck, do boo."

"Okay just making sure it wasn't just me. How they got all of them hoes over there and they can't take their eyes off us?" Thyri replied.

"Probably because they can't bag us. The chicks over there being thirsty as hell and they're checkin' for us. Watch this."

"Hell nah! What you about to do?" Thyri quizzed with a raised brow.

"Don't worry about it. I'm about to do something them broads can't do," she replied calling a waitress over to their table.

Thyri was too buzzed to focus too much on what her friend was doing. She kept taking shots enjoying the show.

Soon as the waitress appeared in the VIP section with food their eyes lit up.

"Look boo," she said nudging Thyri on the arm.

"Bitch I know damn well you ain't send that shit?"

"I sure the hell did because men need a woman to match their fly boo. That shit gone have they nose wide open," she informed her laughing.

No sooner than Thyri looked over at them, two of the cuties came straight to their table.

"Omg, I'm gonna kick ya ass Kamari. Why'd you do that?" Thyri huffed trying to straighten herself up.

"Yeah, I love you too," she replied, kissing her cheek.

"What's up with y'all?" Legend asked, licking his lips.

"Nothing, just trying to enjoy ourselves. How are y'all, handsome?" Kamari told him.

"So, y'all be out here sending niggas food all the time? You got to let us pay you back for that," Deion spoke eye balling Thyri while reaching in his pocket.

"Nah, y'all good," she told him. She was pinching the hell out of Kamari's leg under the table. "We just wanted to feed y'all, you know?"

"Have a seat," Kamari told them.

They chopped it up for a while and after the club closed , they left together and headed to the Waffle House to get food and get to know one another outside a club setting...

CHAPTER NINE

T hyri scrolled her social media, looking for the next set of drama. Everyone swore their lives were perfect until you watched the messiness that was posted online. Shit, since Kane was locked up her life was calmer and more peaceful. Something she didn't have around him.

She had to give it to her girl though. Kamari knew exactly how to help her get over the bullshit she'd been going through, and that was getting the guys at the strip club's attention.

"Good morning beautiful, are you hungry?" Deion asked as he walked into the guest room with a cup of hot coffee for each of them. "I don't know if you like coffee, but I figured this should get us started."

She shyly sat up in the bed and thanked him. "I don't drink it like that, but this headache is saying otherwise," she said, clearing her throat again.

"Don't be shy, girl. It's all good," he told her. "You're welcome."

Thyri couldn't help but feel a little uneasy. Sure, she had some one-night stands but not with a perfect stranger. She looked around the room and she was impressed. The colors and the décor made it feel like home.

"So, um, I don't remember much about last night, but from what I can see, your house is nice," she complimented.

"Thank you, but this my boy Legend's crib. I'm here from Charlotte. I'm just on a mini vacation away from home.

"Oh, that's what's up," she dryly replied.

"Is everything alright?"

"I'm sorry, yeah, my head is somewhere else right now," she bashfully admitted.

"You know nothing happened last night, boo," he told her with a wide grin. "I can tell that you think something sexual happened."

Oh, thank you God, she thought. Lost in the whole idea that she had just pulled a freaky deaky drive by, Thyri never paid any attention to the oversized t-shirt she had on. Looking down, she closed her eyes and tugged at the shirt.

"Wait, how did I get this on?" she quizzed.

"You were faded. By the time we made it back here you got sick and threw up all over yourself," he explained.

"Oh my God, are you serious?" she replied, covering her face in shame. "Ugh, that was a terrible first impression."

"Nah, it's cool, your girl said y'all had a lot to celebrate, so I understand. Besides baby, I'm not like that. I wouldn't take advantage of you like that."

She was so glad that Kamari thought quick on her feet because otherwise, she wouldn't have been able to recover from that.

"I guess I should be going," she politely told him as she finished up her coffee and grabbed her dress from the chair in the corner of the room.

"You don't want to chill and eat? Your girl is already down there fuckin' some food up. My boy has a chef come in and cook twice a week," he told her. "They hooked up all kinds of food. They just dipped out. You're more than welcome to stay."

Deion was digging Thyri and the way she carried herself. It was kind of scaring him because the only one time this happened is when he met Indya. His emotions were all over the place. Everything he did and everyone was reminding him of Indya. He had to be careful not to let his emotions lead him somewhere he didn't want or need to be.

"Well shit, I guess I will stay. No need to be the downer, huh?"

Thyri's head was spinning, and the night before was coming to her piece by piece. She had forgotten that Kamari even came with her. Shit that was going to be her excuse but there was no sense in running now. She was feeling Deion, but she wasn't ready to kick it with him like that, not yet anyway. She quickly got dressed and headed downstairs behind Deion.

"It's about time ya little freak," Kamari teased soon as she saw Thyri.

Thyri squinted her eyes and stuck her middle finger up at her friend. "I'm not you." She giggled.

"Whatever, sit beside me," Kamari urged patting the stool beside her.

Breakfast was cool and they all enjoyed each other's time. The vibes were there for sure until Casha pulled up on bullshit. She started ringing the doorbell over and over banging on the door.

"Damn, who is that?" Thyri asked, unfazed. "Somebody is in trouble."

"Shit whoever it is wants to get in bad as fuck," Kamari said laughing. They were not at all taking the situation serious and why should they those weren't their men, so whatever woman was behind the assault on the doorbell could take that up with one of them.

"Man, that's my crazy ass baby momma! I know she about to be on straight bullshit," Legend huffed as he got up to answer the door. Lord knows he wanted to let her keep knocking but that wouldn't do shit. He knew she wasn't going to leave until he came to that door.

Casha wasted no time talking shit to him she tried busting up in the house, but he stopped her in her tracks.

"Oh, Shandra was right! She told me that she saw you and ya boys leaving the strip club with some bitches. They must still up in be here!"

"Man, go on with all of that. You ain't my fuckin' girl Casha damn!"

"You don't be saying that shit when you're fuckin' me and suckin' on my pussy nigga so open the fuckin' door!" she demanded.

"Look, we ain't got time for none of this so we gone holla at y'all another time. Tell your boy thanks for breakfast and shit but this our que to leave," Kamari told Deion.

"Nah, it's all good. Y'all can stay," he replied. "Man, she be tweaking out."

"Yeah, we're leaving because this is too much and too damn early for drama," Thyri spoke.

"Well, can I get your number? You didn't give it to me last night."

Thyri couldn't help but to blush. "Yeah, hand me your phone," she requested.

Legend was still standing at the door arguing with Casha because she wasn't letting that shit slide. Kamari nor Thyri gave two shits they were leaving so they would need to pause their little argument to let them get by.

When they walked up on the door Casha lost it trying to fight Legend and everything. They smiled in her face and proceeded to the car.

"Bitch! Shorty was mad as fuck! I know she probably wanted to fight our ass, but she was outnumbered, so she took it out on Legend," Thyri said soon as they got in the car.

"Yeah, she doesn't want none of this, but hell he ain't my man so she needs to relax. It's obvious that she doesn't live there."

"You know how niggas do. They're probably still fuckin' like she said that's the only reason she would have to bug the fuck out like that."

"Enough of all that. Did you give that fine ass nigga the goods?"

"Girl hell no, but I thought I did until he told me we didn't. Why you let me get that damn drunk? It was so awkward eating breakfast man."

"I was fucked up my damn self I don't even know how I was able to drive girl."

"That was a wild ass night. Just glad that I didn't have to do the walk of shame alone," Thyri said.

"Walk of shame? I was the only one fuckin'." She laughed and looked down at her gas tank. "Shit, I need to get some gas or we ain't about to make it to the crib."

"Oh well, stop by Great Stops I need to grab a soda or something because my stomach is upside down."

"Thyri, you know I don't speak about the niggas I be fuckin' but Legend fucked the dog shit out of me last night! That's a nigga I can't fuck all the time, or he will fuck around and have my ass acting like his baby momma and I ain't having it," she said clowning.

"I feel you boo, and shit I'm mad I was too fucked up, but it's all good. I'm going to let him knock the lining out soon enough," she replied laughing.

"Anything to get over Kane's raggedy ass!" Ugh, there it was Kamari was bringing Kane up again unwarranted. She hated that everything she done had Kane sprinkled all over it.

As they pulled into Great Stops, they laughed so hard Kamari almost hit the damn gas pump.

"Bitch you must still be drunk," Thyri said laughing.

"Fuck you heffa. Laughing at your silly ass got me like this. I'm very much sober."

"I'll be right back. Did you want something boo?"

"Nah I'm good about to just pump this gas girl."

When Thyri came out the store she was glowing and smiling at her phone thinking about Deion. Don't front y'all know what I mean. I swear it didn't make no sense how much he had her glowing this soon.

The next thing she knew, she was in a full-fledged fight. She didn't notice Lamar's twin sister coming out the store behind her. Hell, she hadn't even seen her in the store at all.

"Bitch, I'm gone kill you! You're the reason my other half is fucked up!" she shouted before swinging on Thyri, catching her completely off guard.

Thyri stumbled forward but caught herself before she hit the ground. She turned around and started throwing every bit of anger she had built up into each blow she delivered to Lamika's face. Kamari looked up from her phone and saw her girl fighting for her life. She hopped out the car so fast she almost fell.

By the time she made it over to them, Thyri had Lamika on the ground, banging her head against the ground. Seeing as she wasn't needed, Kamari tried to break it up, but it was like Thyri couldn't hear her.

"Y'all had better break this shit the hell up and get up out of here! I just called the fuckin' cops!" one of the cashiers said when she came out.

Kamari had never seen her girl this angry, but nobody could afford to get locked up, so she used all her strength and snatched Thyri off Lamika.

"Don't you ever run up on me, bitch!" Thyri shouted as Kamari dragged her off. "I'm gone fuck you up every time, hoe!"

"Get in the car right now! These motherfuckas called 12. We gotta get the fuck out of dodge!" Kamari told her.

"What the fuck! That bitch just ran up on me out of nowhere. I get it, because I'd be pissed if he was my brother too, but damn! Does she not understand that I went through a fucked-up time behind all of that!" Thyri cried, mostly because this fight just forced her to think about everything that she was trying to put behind her.

"That bitch is crazy! Has she not heard about your hands? I mean, like you said, I get it too, but that was just too much. Now she is looking like the elephant man. You beat that bitch like an egg, boo!"

Thyri sighed heavily and looked at herself in the mirror. "Not one fuckin' scratch!"

"Period! Bet that hoe won't do that again."

"If she ever runs up on me in the future, I will send her straight to hell! Fuck out of here," she huffed.

Although it was unexpected, Thyri felt good. It was like a weight had been lifted off her shoulders. She took kickboxing and Karate all her life, so she could fight, but she didn't like to fight at all. She hoped that Lamika would just let this go. Thyri just wanted to put that part of her life behind her...

CHAPTER TEN

When they got back to Thyri's crib, she gave Kamari something to slip into. They took showers and smoked a blunt to relax. They needed something to take the edge off for sure.

"Bitch, that was wild as fuck! Where did that bitch even come from? I swear I looked up from my phone and a split second later you were beating ass!"

"Girl, I don't have the slightest idea. What's so cold is that I didn't even see her in the store at all. I mean, not that I was looking, but you know what I mean," Thyri said, hitting the blunt as hard as she could. She held that smoke in until it choked her.

"Well, I know she won't be doing that shit again. I just know she felt dumb as hell running up on you only to get beat."

"You know soon as someone asks her about them war wounds, she gone try to flip it and say we jumped her or so something."

"I don't care about that. We know the truth," Kamari told her. "The way you handled her I didn't need to step in except to pull you the fuck off her ass."

Thyri was so sick of dealing with drama in her life that it made her sick to her stomach. It seemed like every time she got to feeling better something else came to destroy her. She needed to get a spiritual cleanse or something because something had to give. At this point, she was starting to think her parents were cursed and it came back on her.

After they finished smoking, they were knocked out like newborn babies. After the morning they had, sleep was all that was needed.

———

"It's all good, nigga! Watch this shit! You won't see my fuckin' daughters since you want to be out here fuckin' all these random hoes! Then got the nerve to still think I'm gone let you knock it down raw!"

"Casha you talking all this shit because you think you run me! I don't care if I do still be fuckin' you! You're not my woman anymore! Grow the hell up!!" Legend barked.

They had been in the foyer arguing for over an hour and Deion was sick of it altogether. He retreated to his room and took a shower blasting music through his air pods so that he didn't have to hear them.

Deion got out the shower and took his air pods from his ears and it was quiet.

It's about damn time, he thought too soon, because as quickly as he thought it, the next thing he heard were the sounds of fuckin' he just shook his head at laughed. Finally grabbing his phone to check missed calls, Deion regretted his decision right away. There were more than twenty calls from Indya and countless text messages.

He sighed heavy and made the decision to head back home so there was no need it bothering to call her back. Grabbing his two black duffle bags out the walk-in closet, he went throughout the guest room and bathroom to collect all his belongings.

Once he was done, he sat at the end of the bed and sent Legend a detailed message letting him know that he was leaving but also that he would be back in a week or two. He figured that if he got away more often it could put the spark back into, he and Indya's relationship. Annoying as she was, he loved her very much and his daughter was his world. There was no way that he ever wanted to break her family up.

True indeed he was feeling Thyri, but just a little bit too much for his taste especially that soon, so he was going back home early to apologize.

Finally taking the time to slowing down and looking at the bigger picture he knew that he was doing the right thing. As he drove back home to the Queen City, he had a lot of much-needed time to think.

Finally making it home shortly after noon, he got instantly annoyed. He didn't know why but he felt weird.

"Here we go," he dryly spoke getting out of his Land Rover. He headed inside ready for a knock down drag out. Deion knew that she would be in rare form especially since he hadn't replied to her calls or messages.

No sooner than he walked into the house he turned his nose up. It didn't look like Indya had cleaned up since he left.

Shaking his head, he looked around the house more before calling Indya's name.

"Bae! Where you at? Indya!"

Moments later she came rushing out of the downstairs guest room with a t-shirt on and her hair tossed all over her head.

"What are you doing back?! I blew your ass up all night nigga! You didn't text back or nothing," she ranted.

"Why you in the guest room?" he quizzed with a raised brow.

"Nah, you don't get to come up in here demanding shit! You left this family Deion, not me!" she huffed.

"That's why I came back instead of calling you because I want to fix this shit."

"Oh, now you want to fix it after all the bitches you have fucked around on," Mariah said as she walked from the same room Indya had come out just a few minutes earlier.

Indya knew the gig was up, so she just closed her eyes because she knew that Deion was about to go off the deep end. She needed to think quick on her feet if she was going to stay ahead of Deion.

"What the fuck are you doing here? I didn't see your truck outside," he barked. "The hell y'all got going on?" Deion looked at Mariah with anger in his eyes and malice in his heart he couldn't stand her nor the ground she walked on.

"Fuck you Deion," she huffed.

"Bitch, this is my motherfuckin' house! Get the fuck out!"

"Chill out, Mariah! Damn!" Indya grilled, stepping in between the two of them. "Now is not the time. Can I talk to you?" she asked Deion.

Deion was livid and wanted to knock the lace front from Mariah's head, but he held back. Upon closer observation, he noticed that she was also just in a t-shirt and panties.

"Hold the fuck up! Y'all hoes fuckin'?! Well, isn't this about a bitch!"

"Deion, baby, it's not what you think," Indya pleaded.

"Fuck that, Indya! This nigga stays cheating on you, even bringing bitches up in the house y'all share with Gianna. This man has no respect for neither one of you!"

"Would you shut the fuck up!" Indya spat. "Can you give us some time to talk?"

"Nah, no need to talk now. Shit, Mariah is the player here," he replied, laughing. "Since you got so much mouth, why don't you tell her how you be eating my dick anytime I call you?" he taunted.

"You dirty son of a bitch! You promised," she whined.

Indya's head was spinning out of control, and she lost her balance momentarily. "I know I didn't hear what I think I just heard. So y'all been fuckin' around?!"

"We sure have," Deion said, doubling down as Mariah tried to attack him, but she was stopped by Indya knocking her upside the head.

After laughing and recording the event, Deion decided to break their little cat fight up.

"Bitch! I can't believe you! Always trying to keep me away from Deion when you were fuckin' him the whole time, smiling up in my face," Indya spat.

"Come on boo, you know it wasn't like that. You know when I'm drunk and high my judgment is off. This bastard took advantage of me."

"Yeah, that didn't happen." He laughed, walking away. "I don't give a damn what y'all do for real. I'm getting my shit and I'm leaving! Matter of fact, where is my daughter at?" he snapped.

"You're not going anywhere, Deion! You are just fuckin' getting here! But you can get the fuck out!" she told Mariah.

Mariah knew she had fucked up, so she went and gathered her things while she waited by the front gate for her rideshare.

"Nah Indya you got this. I don't know why you bothered following me because I'm not changing my mind. I came home to get up back on track only to find this shit out!"

"Can we please just have an adult conversation about it then. I mean you do at least owe me that Deion. Considering all the bullshit I've put up with," she replied trying to gaslight him while tears fell from her face.

Deion laughed inward because he knew this tactic all too well. That's the move he typically used on her. *Touché*, he thought, placing the luggage on the bed he flopped down.

"I'm listening." She was right that was the least he could do. Now he was all for his girl liking girls, but he wasn't a fan of that lying shit because although he did what he did, he never lied about anything. Not only that but for the fact that Mariah tried turning them against one another after sticking her claws into them both.

"I know this is the last conversation we should be having but I made a mistake Deion. You know that I would never intentionally hurt you. I was vulnerable because of what me and we've been going through," she whined.

Deion put cocked his head to the side and started twisting one of his locks.

"Damn, you not gonna say nothing?" she huffed.

"Shit, what do you want me to say? This is too much for real," he replied.

"The nerve of your ass to say something is too much! You know what, fuck it leave then we don't need you anyway!!" she yelled standing to her feet pointing at the door for him to leave.

"You're real funny as shit." He chuckled as he left out their bedroom.

"Don't bring your ass back either, nigga!" she spat. "I'm so sick of always begging your low-down, dirty, community dick having ass to treat me right. Fuck outta here!"

Indya loved that man beyond words, but she was sick and tired of his bullshit. Especially since he'd been the one cheating the entire relationship, and now he was breaking his neck to leave over her mistake. Yeah, it had happened over the past year, but he didn't know that. It was just getting to her because he was always nonchalant about everything, never trying to fight for their relationship. After a long conversation with herself, and a few romantic movies later, she decided to try letting him go and hopefully, he'd come back.

Once outside, Deion sat in his truck for a good twenty minutes before pulling off and heading back to the Boro. He hated how his day was going because for once, his intentions were pure, but it was simply too late. He figured that he'd give Indya some space for a while. After shooting Legend a text letting him know that he was on the way back, he hit the highway...

CHAPTER ELEVEN

Thyri was knocked out, calling the hogs, as the old folks would call it. Suddenly, two of the pictures on her wall fell and shattered.

"What the fuck!" she shouted. Her heart raced out of fear of what was going on and her body shook uncontrollably. She sat there quietly for a few minutes and heard it again, but this time she heard her neighbor British screaming for help.

She quickly sprang from her bed and slid her house slippers on with the quickness. She'd been through the same thing, and she wouldn't stand by and hear or see another woman go through that.

By the time she made it to the top of her stairs, she went back to her room as fast as she came out of it.

As badly as she wanted to help the girl, she decided against it. She just knew how overprotective women tended to be behind their abusers and she wasn't trying to deal with that drama. Thyri crept downstairs to see if Kamari was still asleep.

"Girl, why the hell are you creeping down here like a damn lunatic?" Kamari asked as she sat up on the couch.

"Girl, I was trying to see if you were up, and if you weren't I was going to head back upstairs."

"How the hell am I supposed to sleep with your neighbors acting like they live in a house?" she huffed. "That nigga over there knocking her head up against the walls and shit." She laughed.

"I know bitch, they scared me out my damn sleep! I was going to go over there for real, but I decided not to. Lord knows I have my own problems and all, but I know that she ain't gone do shit but protect him, and then I'll have to knock her head between the washer and dryer," she clowned. "I'm not for none of that at all, girl."

"You're a mess, but I feel that because women do that shit all the time. I don't know what life has in store for me but if I ever go through anything like that, I pray I'm one and done. That shit is exhausting."

"That shit is not for the weak at all. Wish I never had to experience that in my life."

Thyri pulled her phone from her robe and checked her socials, but there wasn't anything to see except for a message from Deion's fine ass.

"Yeah, I think I would fold boo," Kamari admitted. "I'm not built for nothing that."

"Shit, I pray you never have to experience it friend. Look I'm about to turn my surround sound on and cook something because I'm overhearing their bullshit. Ahem, that nigga Deion text asking if he could see me later." She giggled.

"Oh shit, let me find out. Not him hitting you up so soon. Now that's tea baby! That nigga Legend probably still beefin' with his baby moms," she replied ignoring what she said about the food.

"Period," Thyri said as she disappeared into the kitchen.

"You better text his fine ass and say yes too!" she shouted.

Thyri looked around when she got into the kitchen and a wave of emotions took over her body out of nowhere. Bracing herself against the counter, she took in several deep breaths and slowly exhaled. She was so thankful to have her life spared because the way Kane was acting before being locked up was on another level of scary.

"Whew, thank you God." She chanted holding her hands in the air. Thyri wasn't sure why she was feeling this was in that moment but after thanking God she made breakfast.

The last thing that Thyri wanted or needed was another man in her life, but she welcomed the distraction and decided to just go with the flow.

Deion got back to Legend's house just as Casha was leaving out, she rolled her eyes as soon as he looked at her.

"I will call you later," she recited kissing Legend on the lips getting into her car.

"Nigga, what the hell are you doing back so fast. I didn't think I would see your ass again for a while." He laughed.

"Man, it's a long ass story. Indya's ass ain't as innocent as she acts," he recited as they walked into the house. "I shot you a text letting you know I was headed back up this way."

"I can only imagine. Shit, my phone is on DND man. I need to check it though and you know you're always welcome here. What you trying to get into today?"

"No worries, I hit that shorty Thyri and asked if I could kick it with her today and she was down. If you want me to, I can tell her to bring her friend that's if you're cool with it."

"Hell yeah, I'm down. I didn't get to vibe with her shorty like I wanted to because of my little situation."

"Nigga you mean your baby mother," he said jokingly. "I heard you clapping cheeks."

"Man, you know how these hoes are. All hell breaks loose unless you put the pipe to them. I just needed to break her ass off a little bit." He clowned.

"You're right about that. I swear the shit is so predictable," Deion replied.

"Fuck it! tell her to bring Kamari. Shit, I think that was her name," he said pretending to forget. Legend was not about to let his boy know that he was a little thirsty.

A few hours later, Deion and Legend arrived at Thyri's condo with two dozen roses one for each of them. Deion got yellow roses whereas Legend got the classic red. They went to the door like gentlemen instead of blowing the horn for them to come out.

When Thyri opened her door, she had to keep her mouth from hitting the floor. She was surprised they even came to the door. Any man she'd dealt with up to this point just tooted the horn.

"Aw, look Kamari." She came straight to the door, and her mouth did in fact drop. Shit she ain't never received a flower a day in her life let alone a whole bouquet.

"Y'all look nice," Deion said.

"They sure do," Legend agreed.

"Thank you," they said in unison. They looked at each other and giggled playfully.

They took their flowers and put them in vases while the guys waited by the door.

"My bad guys," Thyri apologized. "Y'all can come inside."

"It's all good," Deion responded with a wide grin. Thyri couldn't help but blush when she saw his smile. The locs, his tattoos and that smile had her ready to risk it all.

"So, where are y'all taking us?" Kamari asked when they sat down.

"You'll see when we get there Shawty. It's a surprise," Legend told her licking his lips.

Kamari didn't know what it was about this man but every time he licked his lips while staring her in her eyes, her pussy got wet. That's how he was able to knock it down on the first night. She desperately wanted to ask him about his baby moms, but she left it alone. It wasn't her place.

"I hear you," she purred.

Once they all piled into Legend's 2022 Porsche Cayenne Kamari glared at Thyri who was scrolling on her phone.

"Get off your phone. Where you think they're taking us?" Kamari asked in a low whisper.

"Shit, I don't know probably a restaurant or something. You know that is far as niggas minds go when it comes to a date," she whispered back to her friend with a smirk on her face.

"What y'all back there whispering about?" Legend asked positioning the rearview mirror so he could see her.

"Dang nosey," Kamari said giggling. "Maybe it's a secret. You worry about watching the road. Ain't nobody trying to die today."

"We're just trying to figure out what this surprise is sir," Thyri spoke giggling.

"Oh, shit Deion you in trouble my boy. She said sir and every woman I've been around that said sir is crazy! You better be careful with this one." He clowned and they all erupted into laughter.

"Aht, aht, don't do my best friend."

"I'm sure I'll be good in her hands," Deion flirted.

"Wow really?" Thyri managed to say through her laughter. "And trust me you will." Every time she looked at him and his long locs she just couldn't help but smile. He was fine-fine to her. She knew above all else she was going to have to pace herself with him.

"I'm just fuckin' with you Deion and I think y'all will like the surprise. Just sit back and relax. Put it like this y'all won't be disappointed."

They did as he asked and enjoyed the ride while making small talk. When they made it to their destination, they couldn't believe that it wasn't the typical place.

"Oh, shit the Zoo?" Thyri said excitingly.

"Yeah, I love this. I can tell it was well planned out which is a good sign," Kamari spoke.

"We knew y'all would like it," Deion replied.

"We a different breed baby. Niggas out here trying to show y'all something. Don't nobody want to just go out to eat and shit feel me?" Legend spoke.

"Oh, yeah, I feel it," Kamari replied hitting Thyri's leg.

"Y'all wanna smoke before or after we go up in here?" Deion asked.

"Smoke? Hell yeah," they all answered in laughing.

"Say less," he said sparking the blunt he rolled on the way there.

By the time they all made it in there they were faded laughing at everything they saw. After about an hour of talking getting to know one another and nonstop laughing. Deion kept his hand on the nape of Thyri's ass the entire time. While Legend had his arm around Kamari's shoulder. On the outside looking in they could have passed for two very happy couples.

"Thank y'all," Thyri spoke as they headed out the Zoo. "This was a good idea for a first date."

"Yeah, that was lit for real," Kamari said. "I enjoyed myself."

"It was no problem at all," Legend replied.

"I had a good time. Y'all are cool as hell for real," Deion told them.

"Yeah, we hear y'all. This is just one day, but I will say that you guys are doing good as of right now," Thyri told them.

"Damn, tough room," Legend said laughing.

"Nah, we're just guarded. That's what she's trying to say," Kamari told him.

"We get that. Shit, we all been through something. Let us just show y'all a good time," Deion spoke. "That's all we ask."

"Listen it's no worries at all ladies. Y'all know this day ain't over yet though," Legend told them.

"Well, I hope we're getting food because I got the munchies like a motherfucka." Kamari giggled.

"Right. Me too girl," Thyri said chiming into the conversation.

"Yeah, we gone eat too," Legend replied.

They rode with the music blasting. This gave Thyri and Kamari time to gossip a little bit. This when they let each other know how much they were feeling the guys.

"See, that's why I'm glad you let me get you out the crib. Now you might have a new boo babe," Kamari told her.

"Girl please, you know as well as I do. I'm not ready for all that. I honestly don't think I want to be ready," she honestly spoke. "I'm just here to have fun nothing more. Judging by the way his phone kept going off I'm sure he has a girlfriend or something. Which is of course typical," Thyri told her.

"Look, I know this but it's good for you. Nobody said it's going to go further than this. You know chilling here and there just go with the flow. It's good to have someone to take your mind off the madness."

Thyri loved her friend dearly, but she was starting to get on her nerves a little bit. She knew her friend only had her best interest at heart. It was just starting to annoy her, but she wouldn't dare tell her that. She loved her too much to hurt her feelings in any kind of way.

"We're here ladies. Y'all can stop gossiping now," Legend said as he turned the music off.

"Haha real funny," Kamari said clowning.

Thyri just sat there frozen for a few seconds before she snapped herself out of the mini trance. The last time she was there was with Kane of course when they were on good terms, but it took her back for a second. Almost a second too long, but lucky for her she didn't let it ruin her mood.

"Okay, I see y'all," Thyri spoke so that no one would notice her shift in energy.

"You good girl?" Kamari was on it the second she saw her friends head lower.

"Yeah boo, it's nothing," she replied brushing her off.

Legend and Deion got out first and opened their doors for them once again. This was something they weren't used to at all.

A man opening their door. Yeah, okay! These men had the potential to have them open.

"Y'all showing out today baby!" Kamari giggled.

"Nothing like that shorty," Legend replied with a smile. "This is organic and genuine love."

When they got inside of Bourbon Bowl, they wasted no time at all ordering drinks and food.

Soon as they were all seated at the bar, they were given menus. Legend ordered Gutter Ball Nachos and a round of drinks for the Quartet.

The group spent most of their time talking while they ate before they headed to the lane to bowl a few games. Legend and Deion's phones kept going off like crazy until they silenced their phones.

"We need to team up guys verses girls," Deion said speaking up.

"Nah, not tonight. Y'all ain't about to clown us before the end of the night," Kamari replied.

"Don't put that on me boo, I can get down with the best of 'em so it's whatever to me," Thyri boasted.

"So, you got skills, huh?" Deion flirted. "We should be on teams then."

"More than you know." She smiled flirting back winking at him.

"Break it up now and let's play," Legend said.

"Don't do that. I think it's cute." Kamari giggled. "Let them do their thing." She smiled wildly.

Deion was surprised that he was having such a good time with them. His mind hadn't drifted once missing Indya which was something that usually happened when they were away from each other.

Thyri danced up against Deion between turns as Kamari did the same up on Legend. They were all having a good time.

After playing the best two out of three Legend and Kamari finally won.

"I don't hear you talking now friend." Kamari laughed as she gave Legend a high five. "I thought you could get down with the best of them."

"Damn, you gone just let her play in your face like that?" Deion asked with a chuckle.

"What can I say, you can't win 'em all and Deion if you would have bowled as good as you did the first game we could have won," she told him pouting.

"Nah, we won fair and square. Don't be salty it was all in fun," Legend replied. "We beat y'all ass though!"

"Fuck both of y'all," Thyri huffed giving them the finger.

"You know I love you, bookie," Kamari said giggling.

"It's all good boo. I gotcha," Deion said grabbing her into an awkward bear hug. To be honest, Thyri was low-key feeling it though, so she didn't break away too fast.

After, two or three more drinks, they gathered their things and left. Thyri hadn't even noticed that she and Deion was holding hands until Kamari slapped her opposite arm to get her attention and pointed. She just gave her a tight grin as her eyes widened.

This time the seating arrangements were different Deion sat in the back set with Thyri. He wanted to chat her up as they headed to drop them off.

As they arrived at her Thyri's complex the police were leaving, and the ambulance was in front of her neighbors' door.

"He must have fucked her up when we left," Kamari said. "That abusive shit is dead as fuck!"

"I knew it was bound to happen," Thyri dreadfully replied. She didn't know the girl like that, but she sure hated to see her go through that.

"Yeah, that shit not cool. That nigga a coward," Legend said.

"A real hoe ass nigga," Deion spoke. This made Thyri's heart smile. At that very moment she knew she had found her person.

"I hate to run y'all, but them drinks are kicking in right about now so I'm gonna see y'all," Thyri said, getting out the car.

"Hold up," Deion said, fast walking behind her.

"What's up, honey?" she quizzed as she fumbled with her keys to unlock her door.

"I hope we can do this again. I like you and I think you like me, so why not?" he said cockily.

"Yeah man, we can do this again." Thyri blushed.

Before Deion even knew what was happening, he was kissing her passionately on the lips. He almost wanted to run away until he noticed that she liked it.

"I see you, my boy!" Legend yelled out after getting his own kiss from Kamari.

"Alright, I'll text you," Deion told her.

"Okay, that's cool," she replied.

Thyri couldn't believe that Deion had just stolen a kiss like that, but she wasn't mad at him either. The way she saw it, life was too short to play hard to get. They were very grown and had free will, so it was up to all parties to handle the situation the right way...

CHAPTER TWELVE

I ndya was mortified when she learned that Mariah and Deion had been fuckin' around. She should have known by the way their friendship had changed over the past year and some change. In the beginning, Mariah was an advocate for them, but she began hating Deion. Of course, Indya thought it was because her friend was protecting her, but now she knew better. Her heart hurt and she beat herself up for not noticing, but with the constant cheating Deion was doing, their daughter, and work, she didn't have time to peep her so-called friend. *The audacity to say she loves me,* she thought.

Wiping her tears, she quickly showered and headed to her mother's house to get her baby. She knew that Gianna would never betray her under any circumstances. She and her mother had a decent enough relationship and right now she needed someone to vent to. When she pulled up to her mother's house, she wiped her constant tears and headed inside.

"Mommy," Gianna yelled, running into her arms as soon as she walked in the house.

"Hey my pretty girl. What have you been up to," she replied kissing all over her face.

"Gianna, get your tail back in this kitchen and eat your food!"

her mother yelled out. She obviously hadn't heard her come in the house or Gianna scream out for her.

"I got her ma," she spoke as she entered the kitchen with Gianna on her hip.

"What are you doing here?" Pamela asked turning around wiping her hands on her apron.

"Lord ma, it's good to see you too."

"You know what I mean Indya. You said you wouldn't be here to pick her up until Monday. What's wrong?"

"Nothing is wrong. I just missed my baby that's all. Do I need a reason to come and get my daughter?" she huffed getting annoyed.

"You are my child and I know when something is wrong Indya. Is it Deion again?"

No longer able to keep it together, Indya broke down crying while Gianna wiped her tears. She always did her best not to cry in front of her daughter, but she couldn't contain herself.

"Deion is never going to change ma. He's impossible. I want to tell you something, but I don't want you to judge me," she said trying to dry her eyes, but the tears kept pouring.

"A tiger never changes its strips baby, and no one is perfect. You must know what's worth fighting for and what's not," her mother responded. "I'm not here to judge you, so whatever it is, I'm sure it's not as bad as you think. You and that man have been through a lot together. I'm sure y'all will work it out."

Indya was taken aback because to date, this was some of the best advice her mother had ever given her. Pamela was a Godly woman, so she was afraid to tell her everything that had transpired but she told her anyway against her better judgment.

"Sit right here and eat your food baby girl. Me and Granny need to talk," she told Gianna sitting her at the table.

"Lord, it's that bad?" Pamela inquired putting the dish rag down on the counter following behind her daughter.

"It's real bad ma. Deion told me that he and Mariah had been messing around. She was there when he threw her underneath the bus."

"What in the hell?! I cannot believe that he took it there." Pamela sat there shaking her head. "What purpose did he have telling you that shit? He has a lot of balls!"

Indya lowered her head in shame. "He found out that me and Mariah had also been messing around."

"What!" she said standing to her feet.

"See, this is why I didn't want to tell you the whole story," she said through tears.

Pamela didn't utter a word she just paced the floor for a few minutes. Indya got up and went back into the kitchen to check on Gianna.

"Are you finished baby?" she asked her as she put her clean plate in the sink and wiped the Ravioli from her daughter's face. Her heart was still racing.

"I know you're young and still don't know your coochie from a hole in the wall. I'm not judging you, but why her of all people? Now you all's relationship will be messed up forever."

After breathing a sigh of relief Indya spoke up. "To be honest it wasn't expected at all. She was just there for me when I needed it the most. I guess crying on her shoulder all the time weakened me and possibly her as well, and I loved her so much already as my friend that it only seemed natural. I know it isn't right ma, but this is my truth."

"Lord baby. What are you going to do now. Where does this leave you and Deion? Hell, where does this leave all of you?"

Indya was surprised at how her mother was reacting because this wasn't normal for her. She hoped that Pamela wasn't going to use this later to bring up in her face. She was aware that you must be careful of who you vent to because you never know what it will bring.

"Honestly, I don't know. I beat Mariah up. I tried talking to Deion but of course he pissed me off being all nonchalant. What you got in here to eat?"

"You know where everything is at girl. Look, if you care about them the way you say you do then make it right. I can't tell you what to do, but Mariah will be around far longer than Deion's tail! It has been too many years wasted as it is and no proposal. You should have been had a ring."

"A ring isn't what's important. Yes, I love him and would love to marry him, but ma if he can't be faithful to me while in a relationship, why would I even accept a proposal?"

Marriage was something that her mother always pushed on her but there was no way in hell that she would marry an already unfaithful man. She might have been dumb, but she wasn't plum dumb.

"This is your life baby. I just want to make sure that you're happy. I know this is a lot to take in, but you need some time to think. Your bedroom is always open. I think you even have clothes in the closet from when you come over here mad with Deion."

"Thank you. I know we don't always see eye to eye, but I appreciate you so much for hearing me out and not making me feel like trash. I think I will stay here until it's time for me to go back to work Monday. I don't want to be home. Since I got everything off my chest, I might give them a call. I don't know."

"Why don't you treat yourself to a nice meal and clear your head. You are always with Deion or Mariah. Maybe you need to focus on yourself for a while, baby."

"I think I might do that, but you know how I hate to be out and about alone, Ma. Why don't you and Gianna come along? We can make it a girl's night. You know? We can come back, pop some popcorn, and watch movies."

"While that sounds good to me, I think this is some time you need alone."

Indya knew that her mother was right, so she shook her head, agreeing with her. She wanted badly to forgive Mariah and Deion, but she was on the fence. However, she needed to also be honest with herself as well. The truth was, they were all in the wrong. She had a lot to think about and she knew this wouldn't be easy...

CHAPTER THIRTEEN

T hyri sat and prayed deeply. She wasn't into getting therapy or nothing like that because she knew all they would do was give her a bunch of medicine to dope her up, and that was something she wasn't having. She needed to find something organic that could help her cope.

She looked at her phone and decided to unblock Kane's social media account. Thyri didn't know what made her want to do it, but she did. Once she clicked on his page, she saw all the pictures on there that he had of them and their kids. For a minute her heart ached for him, but that was short lived. She snapped out of it quick, and her reality kicked in.

Sighing heavily, she got back off his page and decided that it was time to cleanse her home. She needed to do whatever she could to rid her life of that man. Holding onto him would only cause her pain.

Here goes nothing, she thought...

Thyri cleaned her house from top to bottom, she left nothing undone. Anything that Kane had left or bought for her was being trashed. She didn't want anything in her home that could remind her of him at all. It didn't matter how big or small it was, from the socks he left down to the 65-inch TV he put in the spare bedroom. Everything had to go.

As she cleaned out her bedroom tears welled up in her eyes at the good memories they shared. Thyri didn't want to deal with this, but she knew in her spirit that if she was going to have any happiness, this had to happen. Looking underneath her bed as that was the last place anything could have been left, she found the lock box that Kane kept at her house at the beginning of their relationship. She couldn't believe it was still there after so long. Far as she knew, he took that from her place a long time ago, or at least that's what he told her.

Luckily, she still remembered the code. It was his mother's death date. She was sure that nothing of value was in there since they had been beefing so much, but to her surprise, his grandmother's ring was in there. Her mouth dropped when she saw the appraisal amount. It was nearly 1.5 million dollars. *Holy shit!* she thought while grabbing her chest, flopping back onto the bed. Her eyes nearly popped out of her head.

"This can't be real. Shit, what if it is?" she said to herself. Her mind was blown. She really didn't know what to think.

With all the pain she suffered throughout their relationship, she was about to upgrade her life at his expense. That was the least he could do. She flashed back to the day he'd asked her to marry him two years prior with the same ring. He told her how expensive it was but of course, she didn't believe him because he was always broke and asking her for money.

Thyri had just came from school and Kane had the house decorated with balloons and candles burning all the way up the stairs to the bedroom soft jazz playing in the background. In the room he had all her favorite candy spread all over the bed spelling out will you marry me. Her heart melted and she cried at the jester, but she knew that they weren't ready for all of that. Well, she was ready just not with him.

When she declined to accept the ring, she saw the hurt and disappoint in his eyes. Thyri loved him so much but given the struggles they faced in their relationship it was too great for them to jump into a marriage.

After that day Kane became a demon a different person altogether. She always thought if she had just said yes, if his demeanor would have changed. She wasn't dumb at all, deep within her spirit she knew nothing would have changed.

Once she put the ring up on her nightstand, she then put the rest of the things into a small trash bag and took everything including the flat screen to dumpster. Her first mind was to just give it away, but she didn't have time to find someone to give it to because she wanted everything gone. Besides that, there was no telling what bad spirits were attached to his belongings, and lord knows that she wouldn't want anyone to go through that.

Her condo looked a little different with so many things gone off the walls she sighed heavily glad that she made it through everything the devil had thrown her way and stood ten toes down graciously.

Thyri wasn't big on God before, but she knew that he was looking after her protecting her from harm. The last thing in life she thought she would have to go through was an abusive man. However, he spared her life, so she had to acknowledge him and his presence in her life. She turned on some slow jams and lit some sage.

Thyri finished up and took a long hot shower. Her mind felt so free as the hot water beat her body. It was as if another weight had been lifted from her mind body and soul. She was going to take that ring and open her a business and get a bigger place so she could hopefully get her kids back. They were the only thing that was missing from her life, and she wouldn't be whole until she had them back in the comfort of her own home. She couldn't wait to call Kamari over to show her what she had found.

Soon as she stepped out the shower her phone started ringing. Her face lit up like a Christmas tree when she saw that it was Deion hitting her up.

"Let me find out you are feeling me for real," she said aloud. She cleared her voice and tried to sound sexy.

"Hello," she answered.

"What's going on with you beautiful?" he asked. Thyri blushed because she could tell he was smiling on the other end.

"Nothing much, I just finished cleaning my place." She wanted so badly to flirt and tell him that she had just got out the shower, but she knew how men's mind went left, so she kept that part to herself.

"That's what's up. I really enjoy your vibe and I want to know when I can see you again," he said cutting straight to the chase.

"I mean I have to work for the next couple of days, but maybe this weekend if that's cool with you."

"Yeah, I like that. Me and my boy got some business to handle so that works out perfectly."

"Sounds good. Maybe then we can get to know each other on a different level." Lord knows Thyri didn't want to spill all her tea, but she did want to know more about Deion so that meant she would have to share details about herself as well. Especially if she wanted what they had going on to continue and on a good note.

"Yes, I agree. I hate that we haven't had a chance to do that just yet," he admitted. As of right now that had a few links but never no real conversation about who they were. They had only been talking for a little over three weeks but she was feeling him too.

"Okay, well I hate to cut you short, but I gotta go. Is it okay if I hit you later?"

"Hell yeah," he answered overly eager. He couldn't do nothing but laugh at himself.

"Okay bye love," she said disconnecting the call. She couldn't hardly wait to call Kamari.

Before she had the chance, she called Kamari was ringing her doorbell. She looked at the app on her phone and nearly broke her neck racing down the stairs with the ring and appraisal papers.

"Bitch get in here," she said pulling her through the door still wearing her robe.

"What the fuck is going on?" Kamari asked in a panic. She frantically looked around for any possible threat.

"Girl, sit down," she instructed.

Reluctantly she sat on the sofa with her heart in the pit of her stomach. She didn't know what to expect from Thyri or what she had to tell her.

"Please just tell me girl you got me nervous as hell."

"So, I deep cleaned today and threw anything out that reminded me of Kane I mean I was tossing socks and all. Even that big ass TV that he put in the spare room."

"Okay, and what happened. You're killing me with all this damn suspense," she huffed crossing her arms over her chest.

"Look at this," she said shoving the ring in her face."

"This shit is nice as hell why haven't you ever showed me this?"

"Girl, because I didn't know that shit was still here. After he asked me to marry him, and I declined his off I thought he took it back to his Aunt's house I had no idea that he kept it here."

"Wow, look at God. Sell this shit I know it's got to be worth a few racks," she said giggling.

"Nah, not a few racks bitch! Try 1.5 million motherfuckin' dollars!" she yelled tossing the paper into Kamari's lap. They jumped around screaming and dancing.

"This is not only a blessing boo but God showing you that he got you even when you ain't got yourself," Kamari told her. "Man, this shit is crazy!"

"That's the first thing that came to mind but that nigga ain't about to be locked up for a lifetime boo. When he gets out, he will try and kill me for real this time!" she explained.

"Move out of this bullshit ass condo and he won't be able to find you. I say sell it!"

"I don't know girl. I could always move out of the way but who's to say he won't find me. Shit!"

"Girl, fuck him! Because of his ass you don't have custody of your kids! Everything else is minimal. I mean, I'm not trying to say what he has done to you doesn't matter boo, but he probably doesn't even remember leaving that shit. Especially since he stayed in your pockets."

Thyri thought for a few minutes, going over different scenarios in her head on how she could pull it off without getting caught.

"Girl, do you hear me?" Kamari grilled.

"My bad, I'm thinking, boo. Fuck it! Let's have some drinks to this right here! I'm about to move up to a deluxe apartment in the sky with this," Thyri told her, singing and holding the ring in the air.

"Shit, you can buy a mini-mansion with that boo. I'm moving in with you too," Kamari replied.

The happiness that covered her friend's face made her heart melt. She couldn't be happier for her. Through everything that Kane had taken her through within their relationship, Kamari hoped that this would help her finally put him in the rearview mirror and move on to better things, because she deserved it more than she ever realized...

CHAPTER FOURTEEN

Deion blasted his music all the way back down the highway. There had been minimal conversation between Deion and Indya over the past couple of weeks, but she had been adamant about getting her family back together. Deion wasn't trying to hear that because when he was extending the olive branch her ass broke it and tossed it out the window. The only reason he agreed to go back to the house they shared was because he missed his daughter and was tired of only seeing her on Facetime.

Pulling up to the house, he put his blunt out and exhaled. Indya hadn't been his favorite person lately, but he was tired of fighting with her. It was like the same conversation, but they kept getting the same results. Something had to give at this point.

Soon as he punched the access code into the keypad, Indya opened the door with a wide smile and looked better than ever.

"Damn baby, you look good as hell," he spoke, licking his lips.

"You know how I do," she replied twirling around in a circle.

"Where is my baby?" he quizzed as he eased past the foyer.

"She's in the playroom. Gianna! Daddy is home!" Moments later she came running from the back of the house.

"Daddy!"

"Hey G.G., daddy missed you." He quickly dropped his bags and followed behind Indya to the living room.

"Are you sure you're ready to talk Deion because we need to stop the madness. If not for us but for our beautiful baby girl."

"For once I agree with you. To be honest, I'm tired of fighting. The shit is getting old and it's exhausting. I just want shit to go back to what it used to be." He tossed Gianna in the air catching her over and over. She just giggled trying to get out of his hands. He did kind of bad because he had told Thyri that he and Legend had business to handle, but his family meant the world to him.

"Not what it used to be but us to be better. Deion, I have had a lot of time to think and if you cannot be the man, I need you to be without the cheating then maybe we need to separate."

That hit Deion in the gut so hard he nearly fell from the chair. In a million years he never expected for her to mention them going their separate ways. True enough he'd cheated on her often, but she was always so forgiving once he apologized.

"Daddy, can I do your hair?" Gianna asked in the sweetest voice as she twirled his locs in circles.

"Of course, you can baby," he replied.

"So, you're just going to ignore what I said Deion? She huffed. "See, this why I told you to get out the last time you're always so damn nonchalant when it comes to important matters. Speaking of which, when are you coming back home. I know you call yourself making money with your little friends, but your family is here."

"Whoa, you need to relax. I came in here with positive vibes. You didn't even give me a chance to say anything. I was thinking and the G.G. asked me a question, so I answered her. Ain't nobody being nonchalant Indya." Deion was already regretting coming home soon as she bit his head off for not answering fast enough. He knew he'd hurt her beyond repair, but she was doing too much if he was there, it meant he was trying to give them another shot why couldn't she see that?

"What are you saying Deion?" she urged folding her arms.

"I'm saying you're right okay. I'm all in, baby. If you want us to work, it out I will commit to just that. No bullshit this time," he admitted. Looking down at his phone, Deion replied to Thyri's text with a wide grin.

"Is that a bitch on your phone right now?"

"Nah, that was Legend. If we're going to do this, you're going to have to trust me."

"Trust is earned Deion and you haven't earned that back yet. This shit is like alcoholics anonymous. We will be taking this one day at a time."

"That's cool, but don't assume that a bitch is calling me every five minutes."

"I have known you for years and never seen you smile like that over another man calling you either but whatever Deion."

What's up you are cooking because I'm hungry as hell."

"Wow, and no I'm not cooking we can go out and grab something," she replied rolling her eyes.

"Bet, let me run upstairs and take a quick shower before we go," Deion lied.

"Hey where do you wanna go?"

"I don't care you choose!" he yelled back downstairs to her. When he got into the bathroom, he locked the door and turned the shower on to drown out any sounds before calling Thyri.

"Hello," she whispered into the phone.

"My bad shorty, you busy?"

"I'm at work. Is everything okay?" she inquired with a raised brow. He never called her before without texting first.

"Yeah, everything is good boo. I was calling you since I didn't text you back. You know I wanted to check on your fine ass," he replied.

"Aw, look at you, being a sweetheart." She giggled. "Can I call you back I'm getting off in the next hour?"

"Just shoot me a text. I need to handle this little bit of business," he lied.

"Okay that's fine. Later," she replied disconnecting the call. Deion shot Legend a text letting him know his moves so he wouldn't accidently spill to Kamari. No sooner than he put his phone down and stepped into the shower, Indya was busting up in the bathroom rushing him along.

"Damn girl, I'll be down in a few minutes. You lucky Gianna is up otherwise I'd make you get in so I could break you off. I need to get this stress out."

"I'm sure it's not that much knowing your ass," she sarcastically replied.

"See that's the shit I'm talking about," he barked as he snatched the shower curtain back.

"Whatever Deion just hurry up because now that your daughter knows were going out for food, she is acting like she's about to starve." She walked out the bathroom slamming the door.

Deion hurried up and washed off when he was done, they headed out.

"Oh, my goodness, you smell good as hell," Indya told him gawking at him. "This how I got pregnant the last time."

"Yeah, I remember very well. I was tearing that ass up," he replied laughing.

"Shhh," she urged looking into the backseat to make sure Gianna didn't hear what he said but she was fast asleep. It didn't matter that she had just woke up just before Deion got home. Anytime they took a car ride it was minutes before she would be knocked out.

When they pulled up to King's Kitchen Deion gave her a look of disapproval.

"Why are we here? Don't we need a reservation?"

"Yes, but you know Mariah is the manager. She gave us the hook up bae," she dryly replied.

"You know the last motherfucker I want to see is her ass. Y'all cool again?" he said gritting his teeth.

"We are. Deion can we please just go eat like a family it's been way too long, and I don't feel like doing this right now." He just looked at her with anger in his eyes. This was being done out of spite and he knew that which infuriated him even more because why would he ever want to be around Mariah again after everything she'd caused.

Indya parked her car, turned the ignition off and got out and got Gianna out of her booster seat.

"Are you coming," she asked him.

"Yeah, I'm coming Indya. You think this shit is a game but I'm going to let you live," he replied slowly removing his seat belt.

Mariah greeted them at the door with a wide sneaky grin spread across her face. Deion wanted to wrap his hands around her neck, but he wasn't an abusive man that didn't stop the thoughts running through his mind.

After they were seated Gianna started crying because she was hungry. The waitress came straight over to take their order.

"My name is Arica, and I will be your server tonight. Can I get you all started on some drinks.

"Yes, can I have an Apple Cider Margarita. What you want bae?" she asked him.

"Let me have a Jamaican me crazy and give us an orange juice for this one," Deion replied as he tried to keep Gianna settled.

"Okay, I will be right back with your drink orders," she said walking away.

"Why are you looking like that Deion?"

"It's all good. Nothing to worry about it," he replied giving her a cold stare. He wanted to chew her out so bad, but he wasn't about to give her the satisfaction and he damn sure wasn't about to argue with her with their daughter looking at them.

"Look, I know you're mad about the Mariah thing, but we have talked about everything, and I forgive you both. It didn't come easy, but I did. I need you to understand that she and I have been through so much together even before I met you. I just want us to put this behind us and move forward.

"I get it," he lied. "I mean what can I say about it, Indya?

You're not my property there is nothing that I can say that will change it so can we just eat, and we'll talk about it later."

"I'm glad you said that because I have already text Mariah and she's okay with coming by for us to have a reasonable conversation since that didn't happen the last time, we were all in the same space."

"You know what!? I don't know what the fuck you're on but that shit ain't happening! Y'all can be buddy-buddy all you want but that doesn't mean I have to like her or deal with her for that matter."

"Agree to disagree we're having this talk Deion."

"You got it baby," he replied with a devilish grin. That was the nail in the coffin. He was going back to Greensboro and push his issue with Thyri. He didn't know what was going through Indya's mind, but he didn't get down with Mariah like that especially since he found out she was doing Indya too. He realized in that moment that he had lost the woman that he once loved...

"Please don't hang up," Kane pleaded.

"What the hell do you want Kane?" she spoke through clenched teeth. It had been so long since Kane had tried to reach out to her, she assumed that he was finally going to let her go.

"I wanted to tell you that I'm sorry. I mean it this time baby. Please don't do this to me. We have been through so much shit I can't see my life without you. I know I've done a lot of fucked up shit, but it was all out of love. I will get help or whatever it takes just please don't leave me man. I ain't go nobody," he said through tears. This wasn't anything new with Kane and Thyri wasn't buying it anymore especially since she'd found someone worth her time.

"The only reason you're calling me with that fake crying shit is because you don't want me going to court on your ass. It's crazy because for so long my heart broke every time, I heard you cry because I wanted to believe that the Kane, I once knew was still there but you're a monster. I don't care what you are going through please leave me the hell alone!" she yelled disconnecting the call.

Thyri and been off work from both of her jobs for a little over a week. She needed something better, but she was going to wait just a few more months and she could quit her job at Texas and never look back. She loved it but it was bittersweet. She had both good and bad memories for the time she worked at Texas Roadhouse. She was down to two days maybe three at the hospital which was blowing her. Soon enough she would be done with both jobs especially if the appraisal was good on that ring. She was a little bit scared that Kane would come after her but she was sure he would be locked up for a few years after everything he had pulled in consideration of his record.

The only real reason she wanted to quit her job was because she was tired of people that she knew coming to eat just to ask her a million and one questions about Kane and everything that happened. It didn't matter how long it had been the questions never stopped coming and it was wearing her down she just wanted to snap on everyone that even brought anything up. Thyri didn't care about the people that she was cool with asking her, it was the ones that has never spoken to her at all that pissed her off.

"Good morning, my name is Thyri and I'll be your server. Can I start you with a beverage?" she asked looking up into the cold dead eyes of Lamika. She was sitting there with a gun on her lap.

"Yeah, chop-chop," she barked snapping her fingers. "We want some sweet tea bitch!"

Thyri was mortified her heart was on the ground. She wanted to leave the table and go out to her car, but she held her composure. THyri silently sighed and swallowed hard before she spoke.

"So, because I whipped you up like some cake batter you want to shoot me?" Thyri barked as she iced grilled her dead in her eyes.

"Nah, I ain't gone shot ya ass yet bitch, but you better believe it's coming," Lamika told her.

"Well, why the hell you come in here and put it on your lap? Everybody knows where I live but you came to my job with your little minion over here, I guess trying to check me or whatever this is, but baby, I'm not scared of you and nobody else. Play them games on a hoe with a GED!" Thyri spat.

"I'm not for none of that shit! I'll beat your ass right here and now," the other girl said, attempting to stand up in her face, but Lamika stopped her.

"Look, this was fun, but unlike y'all hoes, I need to get back to work. Find something safe to do, Lamika. This isn't what you want. I know it may seem like it, but if I wasn't at work, this shit would be up," Thyri said, walking away.

"Girl, what was that about?" Nyla, another server, asked.

"Tuh, nothing, just this bitter ass bitch mad at me because her brother got beat up, so she wants to blame me."

"Well, you must have got her shook because they're leaving," she told Thyri, pointing in the direction of the table they were sitting at.

"Yeah, it's all good though. I'm straight. They need to get a life," she replied, walking to her other tables to make sure that her customers were good.

Deep down she was petrified when she saw the gun on Lamika's lap, but she couldn't let her see her sweat. She knew she had to stand her ground if she was going to walk away unscathed. All she knew was that this would be the last time Lamika caught her lacking...

CHAPTER FIFTEEN

When Deion woke up to head the next morning, he wasn't complaining. He sat upright and sparked his blunt that was sitting on the nightstand. Taking a deep breath of the blueberry Kush, he slowly blew it out while taking his hand to push Mariah's head down his thick shaft. Indya was behind her, licking her wetness as it poured from between her legs like hot lava.

"Fuck, don't stop," he moaned in pleasure.

"Mmmm, you like that?"

"Yeah, now don't stop," he demanded. "Eat this dick!"

Deion looked up and Indya was sticking her tongue out her mouth, letting spit drip from it into Mariah's ass. She blew a kiss at him and bent down to lick it up, which made his dick jump.

"Get up," he told her. "Come here, bae." He bent Indya over and rammed all nine inches into her from the back. He placed his hands on her ass like he was gripping a basketball and pumped vigorously while he sucked on Mariah's breasts.

"Yes daddy, fuck me harder," she panted out of breath, grabbing at the sheets. "I'm about to cum, Deion." He couldn't hold his nut in any longer. He busted up in her so hard that he almost collapsed.

"God damn, that was fuckin' amazing," he said, falling on the bed.

"See baby, I told you we can make this work."

Deion wasn't open at all to having a conversation with Mariah in the beginning, but by the time the night was over, they were both all over him and he couldn't resist. The drinks they had mixed with the weed had him in another world.

Knowing that this was a tactic to keep him around, Deion wasn't sure how he felt about what they had done. Nothing would ever be the same after that, and Indya was too territorial to let that happen too much. It didn't matter either way to him because it was strange to him anyway. Hell, it took the fun out of sneaking around. This whole ordeal made him want to change his ways. He hated that Indya felt like she had to do that in order to keep him. Although he busted some of the best nuts, he had in years it was somewhat of a turnoff. He should have known something was off when she didn't go off the deep end when he had the last shorty in the house when she came from her business trip. That was the day he just knew he was going to lose his life. Hell, she acted worse than that when she found out that he was fucking around with different females. It was just beyond him how they had gotten here.

"I'm going downstairs to shower. I have to get to work in an hour," Mariah announced as she grabbed her clothes off the floor and left the room.

"Okay, well call me later," Indya replied. Deion just stared at her, trying to figure out what she was thinking.

Deion sat on the bed scrolling through his phone and Indya looked at him confused.

"What's wrong?" she quizzed.

"Nothing, just checking my social media."

"So, what's up baby? Did you enjoy your night?" Indya climbed back in bed beside him. "I know you wasn't expecting nothing like that but I wanted to surprise you. I was reading something online where they said it's always good to be spontaneous with you partner. You know to keep it spicy in the bedroom. I was thinking about some role playing, but I didn't know if you would be into that."

"Yeah, I had a good time. It was different and shit I didn't know you would be into a threesome otherwise I would have been asked you for one," he told her side eyeing her.

"If you would have asked me a year ago, I would have probably slapped you. To be honest I can't believe myself. Are you hungry? I think I'm going to order something. I'm still hungover a little bit."

"Hell nah, I'm about to hop in the shower," he replied getting off the bed.

"You want some company?" she flirted. "I could use a round two."

"Shit, y'all drained my ass. I need to get some life back into myself."

"Well, if you change your mind then I'm ten feet away."

Deion always wanted to have a threesome but he for sure didn't think he would be having one with his girl and her best friend. It was just weird to him the whole dynamic was throwing him off.

After he finished his shower Indya was cleaning the bedroom with the music blasting. He sighed heavily and went up behind her and kissed her neck. He needed to butter her up because he was about to give her an excuse to go back to Greensboro. Deion wasn't mad at her for the threesome he just felt awkward and didn't know what to say to her.

"Mmm, does this mean you're ready for round two?"

"Not quite," he replied. "I need to run back out to the Boro, Legend need me to make a run with him and he don't trust nobody but me."

"Well, who was helping him with shit before you came out there? You just got home Deion. Why you gotta leave? I had plans for us tonight," she whined folding her arms.

"I know baby, and I'm sorry, but I'll probably be back either tonight or in the morning baby," he lied, kissing her on the lips with passion. He was laying it on extra thick.

"Ugh, I guess man, but you better come back, Deion."

"I promise, baby." He kissed her again and left the house with nothing but Thyri in mind. This woman had him in a chokehold and he didn't mind it at all...

CHAPTER SIXTEEN

"So, what's up boo, when you gone try to hawk that damn ring? Because that is the only thing left tying you to that crazy nigga," Kamari asked her.

"Girl, did you forget that I have two kids with that fool? As unfortunate as it is, he will forever be a part of my life and I don't plan on getting rid of it until I can get myself all the way together," she admitted. "I'm trying to make sure I have a plan for that shit, so I don't blow it."

"You are together, girl. Stop doubting your growth, babe. I still can't believe Lamika called herself rolling up at your job like that," she said, changing the subject.

"She ain't on none of that shit. That's why she came to my job, because otherwise, she would have just caught me at the club or some shit."

"If you say so, but I don't trust her at all. It's already clear that it isn't your fault that her brother got beat like that. I mean, shit, the nigga kidnapped you but obviously, she's not comprehending that at all. I just can't lose you, so that shit be on my mind heavy," Kamari told her.

"You ain't about to lose me, girl. She only showed out like that because she had her minion with her. That girl doesn't scare me not one bit. Plus, I got my strap. I'm not worried about her ass."

"Look, you're a grown ass woman, just be careful because strap or not, you can't take that shit inside your job, crazy ass."

"Okay mama, I hear you," she said scratching her head. "Do you want to get something to eat? I ain't trying to dwell on this shit."

"Now you know I can eat, but before I agree to go with you. You ain't been talking about that nigga Deion? What's up with y'all?"

"He straight." She smiled trying to play it off.

"Really? You just gone give me that dry ass response?" Kamari grilled.

"Yeah Kam, I like him, but make no mistake I'm not on him like that," she lied.

"Hoe, lie to somebody else. It's all on ya grill." Kamari laughed.

"Whatever, we going to eat or what? You are doing too much talking," Thyri huffed. "Have you heard from Legend."

"Girl please his baby momma probably chasing his ass all over the triad as we speak," Kamari said laughing.

"I swear you a fool girl," she said laughing. "You're driving too. Where do you want to go boo?"

"It's doesn't matter for real. I'm just trying to eat and chill," she replied. "I'm not driving girl. I can't do it."

"Let's go to Fat Tuesday boo, I want one of them frozen cocktails."

"Oh yeah, that sound good they're so fire and I need something to kill this hangover," Kamari replied.

"Ain't nobody tell your ass to go so hard last night. You saw Jay and started throwing them Casamigos shots back," Thyri said laughing as she blasted her music to drown her out.

"Now you wanna blast the music!" she yelled giving Thyri the finger once she turned around.

When they made it to Fat Tuesday Thyri saw one of her foster sisters.

"Hey bitch! How you been I haven't seen you in years. Oh, my God give me a hug!" Alisha said coming from behind the bar.

"Hey girl! Yes, I know it has been forever. How are you?" Thyri asked with a tight grin looking at Kamari with a side eye the whole time.

"Hey Kamari," she spoke as soon as she stopped hugging Thyri.

"Girl, you know I don't like you," Kamari huffed turning her head.

"Stop that." Thyri playfully slapped her arm.

"Anyway boo. I'm dancing over at The Treasure Club you need to come out there and turn up I'll get y'all in VIP boo even your mean ass," she told them.

"Wow, we were just out there not too long ago, and we didn't see you," Thyri replied.

"I was probably off I only dance a few hours unless I get some side action, you know?" She laughed. "My stage name is Tasty boo, just ask for me, but I gotta go to run my man is out here to pick me up."

"I just bet you do. Freak bitch!" Kamari gritted.

"Anyway, it was good seeing you sis," she said before giving Thyri another hug. "She gave her-her number and left.

"Bye," Kamari said throwing her hand up shooing her away. She couldn't stand her and didn't have a problem reminding her.

"Ugh, she would be a damn stripper," Thyri sighed.

"I don't know why you even entertained that fuckin' gutter snipe," Kamari huffed and ordered them some drinks.

"You know I have a soft spot for her boo."

"Fuck all of that! You should have lost that when she stole all your shit and let Nate fuck her! She knew that was your high school sweetheart! I mean if nothing else she knows you had his baby. Please, I don't like her ass and never will!"

She knew Kamari was right, but they had bonded because

they both lost their parents in similar situations. Thyri wanted to hate her, but it was so hard. However, if she ever crossed her again, she would fuck her up, it didn't matter how big or small.

After their drinks were made Thyri drank half of her cocktail before she even said anything to Kamari. She wasn't mad in the least she just knew her girl was most likely right. However sometimes life was for you to learn on your own with no one else's help.

"It's all good boo. I know it's all out of love," Thyri told her.

"I'm just saying. Anyway, fuck her this is a girl's day for us. Well, evening because it's damn near eight o'clock ugh. Why you let me sleep all day girl," she complained.

"Girl, I took the damn PM's after we left the club, so I was knocked out too. It's all good God knew we needed that rest. That's all."

"Excuse me, can I get two more of these?" she requested.

"Put them on my tab," they heard a deep voice booming from behind them. They looked at each other and turned around to face none other than Deion and Legend showing all their pearly whites.

"Lord, it looks like you seen a ghost," Deion said laughing.

"Sorry, are we interrupting?" Legend quizzed.

"No, y'all just caught us off guard," Kamari told them. Thyri pinched her leg so hard she nearly jumped off the bar stool.

"Hey y'all," Thyri said still gazing into Deion's dark brown eyes.

"She finally speaks." Legend clowned.

"I thought y'all were still out handling business boo," Thyri said with a slightly raised brow.

"Yeah, shit we got back not too long ago," Deion told her.

Legend just shook his head and chuckled a little bit. He knew where his boy was, and he was handling business alright. *These hoes will believe anything,* he thought.

"Let me holla at you," he said pulling Deion to the side.

"Damn, I wonder what that's about?" Kamari quizzed.

"Girl, I couldn't careless," Thyri replied taking a sip of her drink.

"Aye, what all did you tell shorty?" Legend asked.

"Shit, I just told her we had business to handle."

"Oh, okay cool. You know I had to make sure, so I don't slip up."

"Say less and trust me I wasn't about to let you."

"So, what are you beautiful ladies up though this fine Saturday evening?" Legend asked as they walked back over to the bar.

"Nothing. We just came up here for their frozen cocktails and a little something to munch on," Thyri replied.

The last thing we expected was to see y'all, she thought. She was feeling the vibes, but she was supposed to have this time with her friend.

"We came up in here for real to grab something to go, but if it's cool, we would love to sit here and kick it with y'all," Deion spoke.

"Hell yeah. Y'all good if y'all paying," Kamari told them, sucking down the last bit of her second cocktail.

"Come on now, you know better than that," Legend told her as he sat beside her.

"How you are doing, pretty lady?" Deion flirted.

"I'm good, handsome," she replied with a wink. "What about you?"

"I don't have any complaints, baby."

Although she was slightly irritated, she didn't let them know. It didn't matter to her because she enjoyed their company. Besides that, they were a beautiful distraction for her and her girl...

CHAPTER SEVENTEEN

Today was the day that Thyri was going to try and get rid of that ring. She woke up with money on her brain. So much so, she called out of work. Truth be told, if it wasn't for the bills she would have been quit. She wanted to pursue a job in her field but her feelings about being in the medical field had changed since she and Kane started having their problems. She didn't know why, but they had.

Thyri got out of bed and rolled herself a blunt and hopped on social media. She scrolled down her timeline and saved a few funny memes that she could share. She wasn't big on social media but since she had a newfound wealth headed her way, Thyri knew she would have to get active if she wanted to open a business and have it be successful.

When she checked her notifications, she had a few people who had sent her friend requests, and low and behold, there was one from Alisha. She sighed heavily because Kamari's voice was ringing in her head.

"That girl is bad news, boo."

Thyri added her anyway after kicking that little angel off her shoulder. Truth be told, Alisha always had some drama going on and she wanted to be front and center.

What's the worst that can happen? Thyri thought.

She hadn't posted on her page in weeks, so she posted a meme that said, "When things go left, I go to right...to the liquor store." She busted out laughing again as she posted it.

Just as she was about to put her phone down, she got a call from Deion.

"Oh, this nigga is bugged out, but I'm loving it!" she said aloud.

"Hello." She smiled.

"Good morning, pretty lady," he replied. "I hope you slept good."

"I slept okay, I guess. What about you?"

"Yeah, me too," he admitted. "Look, if you're not busy today, I really would like the opportunity to kick it with you, just me and you, feel me."

"Yeah, I remember you was supposed to do that sir, but we ended up running into each other instead." She giggled.

"My bad about that. Shit was so crazy for real. My intentions we're to call you but it went left. If you allow me to, I want to make it up to you," he told her.

"Mmhmm, I guess I'll let you make it up to me," she said through laughter.

"Oh, that's funny to you?"

"Nah, I'm just messing with you. Relax love. Give me a few hours I need to run some errands and I'll be free after that," she told him.

"That's cool with me that way I can find the perfect place for us to go," he said with a slight chuckle.

"Okay it's a date. I'll shoot you a text when I get back."

"Alright, bye beautiful," he replied.

"Bye," she said disconnecting the call.

Thyri blushed so hard after they hung up because she never had a man to call her beautiful so much. It was so refreshing to her. She got out the bed and laid her something casual out to wear. She wanted to call Kamari and have her come along, but this was something she needed to handle alone.

Once her clothes were laid out, she called her case worker. Thyri had been putting it off because she was nervous. Kane was indeed out of her life, but she needed to make sure that she didn't spin that deadly block again. The last thing she wanted was for them to have a problem with that because up to this point she had always had problems getting visitation, so she just let it go until she had her life in better shape. I wasn't like he'd been sentenced yet so she didn't know if they would use that against her.

"Hello," her case worker Samantha answered.

"Hey Samantha, this is Thyri Jacobs. I know it's been a while since we last spoke. The reason that I'm reaching out today is because I would like to move forward with getting my kids back. I would also like to possible be reunited with my first daughter," she explained.

"Hello Ms. Jacobs, I completely understand your concerns. However, as we have previously explained. Your first child has a great foster family, and we are here for the best interest of the child."

"Hold up, so are you telling me that the best interest of the child isn't to be with their mother?" she spat. Thyri was fuming. She was sick of hearing the same shit over and over.

"No, that isn't what I am saying at all. It has been years since that happened and as for the other two, you won't be able to get them back until you and their father are no longer in the picture. I like you Ms. Jacobs but the truth of the matter is that your home isn't a safe environment," she explained.

"First of all," she huffed and quickly calmed herself down because she was about to give Samantha the business. "Yes, I am aware of the situation. Again, as I stated I would like to move forward, and their father is locked up. I thought you all would have found out about it by now, but I guess not."

"Well, we don't know that kind of information unless you notify us," she stated.

"I wish I would have known that," Thyri replied.

"I can't make any promises about that, but I will speak with my supervisor soon as she comes into the office tomorrow."

"Okay, thank you I appreciate that. Goodbye," she said disconnecting the call.

God if you never grant me another prayer for the rest of my life, please let me get my babies back, she thought.

Thyri took her shower and decided not to go out driving around trying to find a jeweler to buy her ring. She just called around instead. She instantly became annoyed because the place listed on the original appraisal was closed for the next three days.

After she called about five other ones, she called it a day. They weren't offering her nothing compared to the price. Thyri decided to do more research online before she tried to sell it for pennies on the dollar.

She knew Deion wanted to take her out, but she decided to cook for him instead. Thyri called him to make sure he was still down.

"Hey beautiful," he greeted as he answered the phone.

"Hey you," she replied. "Okay, so I'm calling because I wanted to know if you just wanted to come over here to my place and I'll make us some food."

"Oh, now that I can get with that. I was having trouble finding a decent place for us to go anyway," he told her.

"Good. Are there any foods that you don't like or maybe allergic to?"

"No ma'am. Whatever it is that you make I know I'll love it."

"Okay, cool. Well slide in about an hour love," she replied.

"See you then."

Thyri hung the phone up and headed straight into the kitchen. It had been so long since she cooked for anyone besides her and Kamari, she had to double check to see what she had.

"Ugh, brunch it is," she said to herself when she realized that all she had was breakfast food.

Thyri pulled everything out that she needed to make her

famous French Toast Casserole. She put her playlist on and went to work.

Just as she was pulling it out the oven, Deion rang the door-bell. It startled her a little bit until she remembered that he was coming.

"Hold on here I come!" she yelled out.

She looked at herself in the full-length mirror in her hallway before she opened the door.

"Hey there handsome," she greeted with a wide grin.

"Hey beautiful," he replied passing her a single white rose.

"Thank you," she shyly replied as she sniffed the rose. "Come on in, honey."

"Damn girl, let me find out you can cook. You got it smelling like a five-star restaurant up in here," he said.

"Thank you. You can have a seat," she instructed as she headed back to the kitchen. "Make yourself at home."

The last time Deion was at her crib he didn't notice how nice her place was. He smiled that she had the lights dimmed and candles lit.

Thyri came back into the living room with Deion a plate of food and some 1800 since that was all she had.

"Here you go. You could have turned the TV I just had this playing.

"Thank you this looks good, and I love this show," he replied taking it from her. Thyri returned to the kitchen to get her food.

Deion took no time to dig into his food he was starving.

"So, Deion since we're alone. Tell me more about you. I mean it is a little late but what the hell," she said laughing.

"Yeah, we kind of just skipped over the real introduction but it's all good we can do that now. As they say, it's better late than never. What would you like to know?"

"I don't know man. Just tell me what I don't know about you duh."

"I mean there isn't much to know about me honestly. You can see that I'm a laid-back chill dude. In the past I had a gambling addiction. I have a three-year-old little girl. She is my world," he said with a smile spread wide on his face. Thyri could tell by the look in his eyes that he loved his daughter.

"Awe, kids are so amazing," she replied.

"Yes, they are. Do you have kids?" he asked sipping his drink.

Thyri was reluctant to answer him because she didn't have them and wasn't feeling the follow up. "Yes, I do but they're with my family right now," she lied.

Deion wanted to push the issue in asking why they wasn't with her, but he didn't this was something fresh but if they got closer, he would of course want to know more details.

"Are you still with your daughters' mother?" she inquired.

"I wouldn't exactly say that." He told her feeling uneasy. "We're cool, but it's been over for a while now."

"Why stay if you all aren't happy?" she inquired looking at him suspiciously. Thyri was no fool. If a man was saying what Deion said, then chances were that they were still together. Of course, she still wanted to know.

"Honestly, it's because of our daughter. I guess I've been hoping that shit will change but it isn't," he admitted.

"I get that, I mean things don't always work out the way you want them to. You fall in love with your who you think is your person and they change. It seems unfair."

"I couldn't agree with you more. Do you want more kids?" he quizzed. Thyri nearly choked on her drink.

"I really haven't given it any thought, but I guess if the right person comes along and if it's meant to be, it will happen. What about you?"

"I want at least ten kid's man. I love being a father. I was robbed of my father when I was younger. He was a victim of gun violence right here in Greensboro."

"Wow, that is wild man. I'm so sorry to hear that. I didn't know you use to live here. I lost both of my parents in a tragic car accident." Thyri skipped right over the part where he mentioned having ten kids because that had nothing to do with her.

"Whew, I see we have a lot of traumas in common and yeah, I lived here until I was almost fifteen. Then we left after my father was killed. Sometimes I wish we never left," he told her.

"Ugh, don't say it like that. It makes it sound bad. I've learned that life is one big tragedy with good moments. I just want to be happy I have had enough bad days to last me a lifetime," she told him.

"You're right, but it's up to us to make the best of it. I was only supposed to be out here for a minute, but I think I have a reason to stay," he replied with a wink. "Of course, my business is in Charlotte, so if I decide to stay that will all change."

"Whattt, let me find out that you want to stay because of little ole me." She giggled. Thyri didn't want to spill her own tea just yet because she was too afraid that she would run him away.

"I had plans on it for real, but you were the bonus."

"Ahem, let me put these dishes in the dishwasher." She got up and headed to the kitchen.

When she disappeared Deion's phone started dinging. He pulled it from his pocket and saw ten or more photos of Gianna.

"Looking just like her father." He smiled hearted the pictures and texted Indya back before Thyri came back into the room.

"Kiss my baby and tell her I love her. I'll hit you later. Shit is crazy out here."

Thyri came back with some more drinks and fruit for them to munch on. They talked for hours getting to know one another. Thyri's body was so relaxed she didn't know whether it was the weed, drinks or the fact that she was able to vent to someone other than Kamari, but she was enjoying the feeling.

In an awkward silence during a pause in their conversation, she picked her phone up, but Deion wasn't having it he eased her phone from her hand and sat it on the table.

"What are you doing?"

Not saying a word, he pulled her close so he could kiss her luscious lips. She melted in arms every time he touched her.

Whatever he was doing to her it was working because she was starting to fall for him. Real bad. The thumping sensation coming from between her legs wouldn't allow her to resist him. The way he touched her was so delicate and calming.

Finally letting her guard down just a little bit, Thyri straddled Deion, he slowly and enticingly pulled her shirt off while they continued to kiss passionately. Lost in her completely, Deion's dick started growing bigger and bigger. The next thing they knew they heard a bunch of yelling.

"Yo, is somebody yelling your name," he quizzed looking around.

"I don't think so," she replied, getting up to look out the window. She spotted Lamika's Camry right away. Thyri threw her shirt on as fast as she could.

"Thyriiii! Bring your scary ass outside!" she yelled, and gunfire followed.

"Oh shit, what the fuck!" Deion yelled, taking cover.

Thyri dug into her sofa and grabbed her strap. She opened the door and started shooting back, hitting Lamika's car several times before she sped off.

"Stupid ass bitch!" Thyri barked, slamming her door.

"Yo, what the fuck just happened? You ain't tell me I was sitting on a fuckin' gun! Why the hell is some broad shooting at your crib?" he gritted.

"It's a long story, man. She blames me for her brother getting beat up," she told him as she tucked her gun back under the couch pillow.

Deion couldn't believe his eyes. This wasn't what he had in mind when he asked to spend time with her. He knew some crazy broads, but most of them carried knives or razor blades not guns.

"Damn, I ain't know you got down like that," he said in awe.

"Nah, I don't, but I do keep a gun just in case. I am a single woman, so I got to stay protected. I'm sorry about that. This girl has been harassing me for the longest. She refuses to let it go. Maybe I should reach out to her brother and apologize, but he has me blocked on everything. I...I'm sorry you had to see that shit, but that hoe keeps trying me."

"Shit, you don't have to apologize to me. Just remind me to never get on your bad side," he said laughing. "Come here."

At first Deion was spooked out by the random gunfire, but that shit turned him on like a motherfucka.

Let me find out I met my match, he thought...

CHAPTER EIGHTEEN

Deion ended up staying over Thyri's house that night. After turning their phones on DND, they fucked, made love, and tore a hole in the bed. It was like they couldn't seem to get enough of one another. Thyri was in Lala land. It had been a long time since she woke up in a man's arms. The genuine affection was refreshing and welcomed.

After Lamika came over her crib dumping, she was sure that would run Deion off but surprisingly enough, it didn't.

Deion felt her moving around a little bit and he knew that it was go time. He pulled her closer, pulled her thongs to the side, and eased into her walls.

"Ahh shit," she moaned. Deion grabbed her by her face and pulled her head back until it met his, then he bit her ears. As soon as he heard her gasp in ecstasy, he stuck his tongue down her throat.

"Yeah, throw that shit back, baby," he said in a low whisper, grabbing her by the neck.

"Ohh, Deion, ahh."

"You like that, baby?" he whispered into her ear.

With each thrust Deion was punishing her. He couldn't front, she was giving Indya a run for her money.

"Fuck, girl," he moaned, about to nut.

"Not yet, baby." Thyri stopped him in his tracks and turned around and put him in her mouth.

"Got damn, Thyri. Fuck yeah! Just like that," he said, grabbing her hair. "I'm about to cum, baby." This turned her on more and she sucked his dick like it was the last one she would ever have, causing him to explode down her throat.

She sat up, biting her bottom lip. "Nigga, you gotta get out." She giggled. "You about to have me out here crazy."

"Fuck all that! I can't remember the last time I felt so good. I'm gone keep it a bean with you. I don't like sharing."

"What is that supposed to mean?" she teased knowing exactly what he was trying to say.

"You done wore a nigga down," he said sitting up.

"Don't do that. You the one that's been cutting up boy."

Sighing heavily, he checked his phone as she disappeared to the bathroom.

Deion was relaxed more than ever. This woman had a hold on him that Indya never had. Even with the threesome they had something was still missing with he and Indya. He couldn't quite put his finger on it, but something was off he did feel guilty for not being the man Indya needed him to be.

"Come on, get in with me," she said peeping into the room.

"Shit, say less baby." Deion got up and let the sheets fall from his sexy chiseled body.

No sooner than he got in the shower they were back at it again. This was dangerous in so many ways but he was with it.

No sooner than they stepped out Thyri's doorbell and phone was going off like crazy. Her heart dropped the last thing she needed was for Kane to be out of jail popping up at her house. That was it, she had to move from that condo sooner than later.

"Damn bae, is you expecting company or some shit?" he grilled with a raised brow.

"Hell nah." Thyri nervously grabbed her phone. Deion

laughed once they found out who it was. Their best friends came ready for war.

"You got it, go let them in boo," she told him as she started getting dressed.

"This ya spot boo." Of course, since he knew who it was, he grabbed the door.

"So, this where y'all been?" Legend said walking up in the crib.

"Right! These fuckers are in here laid up!" Kamari said laughing. "Got us worried like we're y'all parents and shit."

"Don't do that boo," Thyri said laughing as she came downstairs.

"Girl, the fuck you mean. We been looking for y'all this whole time and you know how I worry about you."

Thyri looked over to Deion and they laughed in their friends faces.

"We love y'all boo," Thyri spoke, and she and Deion laughed again.

"So, it safe to say y'all are feeling each other? I mean laid up ghosting us. Shit y'all had better be at the point," Legend said.

"Come here," Kamari huffed grabbing her friend pulling her to the kitchen.

"Girl, what are you on right now?" Thyri quizzed. I'm okay you're overreacting."

"You know you're my baby TT. Are you sure this is what you want to do babe? You have been through so much and I don't want to see you hurting again behind no nigga, and lord knows when that crazy ass Kane will pop back up."

"Kamari, I could never ask for anyone better than you, but I promise I know what I am doing. Deion is that nigga. No matter what I have been through he makes me feel safe girl," she admitted. "I haven't felt this safe since my I was a little girl. I don't know it feels right."

"I love you girl so whatever it is that you choose then I'm going to hold you down regardless."

"Trust me boo. I got this."

"Thyri, we been though the fuckin' worst but you know I will forever have your back just be careful. I like Deion a lot, but men are men."

Thyri smiled and gave her friend a tight hug.

"I love you girl."

"I love you too, Kamari. I couldn't ask for a better friend boo," she said kissing her on the cheek.

"Shit, I'm just glad you're happy. After dealing with Kane, I didn't think that shit would be possible. That man broke you to no end. I know I've never said it before, but he got what's coming to him."

"Tuh, don't I know it," Thyri replied. "Anyway, let's leave this conversation in hell where Kane should reside for eternity."

When they joined the guys in the living room, they were already blazing a blunt.

"I got some 1800 y'all want a shot and we can get this little party started," Thyri asked.

She came straight back into the living room with drinks glasses and a deck of playing cards.

"Who trying to get spanked in a game of spades?"

"The last time we played a game y'all lost miserably," Kamari teased.

"Girl, that was just luck! Nothing more," Thyri replied, sticking her middle finger up.

"Whatever, just sit down and take this L, boo."

"Not happening today, stink," Thyri told her.

"Oh, we for sure about to smack y'all," Deion said.

"You know what it is my boy," Legend said. "Put your money where your mouth is."

As much as Deion didn't want to bet his friend, he couldn't help himself. It had been too long since he gambled. It was like an itch that needed to be scratched.

"Fuck it! Let's do it," Deion replied dropping five hundred on the table.

"Well damn. Y'all trying to do it big, huh?" Kamari spoke. "Thanks for putting the pressure on us."

Just then Deion got a call from Indya's job phone number.

"Aye, I got to take this call," he told them excusing himself.

"Hello, is everything okay?"

"Yeah, I just haven't heard from you Deion. You said you was going to call us back last night," Indya replied.

"I told you shit was crazy out here man. My bad I didn't mean to ghost y'all," he lied.

"I hear you, when are you coming home. I thought we were working in the right direction, but you keep running to Greensboro every five minutes. I hope after everything you're not still on your bullshit," she grilled speaking in reference to their threesome with Mariah.

"No, man chill. You're always jumping off the deep end. I'm out here making some extra money. You know my business is slow and I would be less than a man if I allowed my woman to take care of me," he explained laying it on thick.

"So, you're not mad about all of that?"

"If I'm being honest, I don't know how to fell about the whole ordeal. I never even knew you got down like that in all the years we've been together, then on top of that we all join the party. Yeah, Indya I'm at a loss for words." Dein wasn't lying to her because that was how he felt but having Thyri made it easier to just let she and Mariah have one another because that shit wasn't going to work no matter how badly they wanted it to.

"Wow," she replied. After a long pause she broke her silence. "Why didn't you just tell me how you felt the next day Deion? I don't know how much it would have changed things, but we could have figured it out together. Indya knew that she was taking a risk when they done it, but she was also hopeful that their relationship or at least their communication would get better but not even that happened.

"I didn't want to hurt your feelings. I know that it meant a lot to you and while I appreciate the freak session it just wasn't what I expected."

"Nigga, are you trying to clown me," she huffed. "You really are a piece of shit Deion. I don't know why I've stayed with you for so long. I deserve so much better!"

"God damn, Indya why must you always go from 0 to 100 over the smallest shit?"

"Because you have cheated for most of our relationship, and I have stuck by your side. Shit, what nigga wouldn't be more turned on by having a threesome? You're a weirdo!"

"Aren't you at work? Why are you yelling like that? The partners must be out of the office," he taunted.

"Yeah, that's right, they are, but you have pushed my last nerve, Deion! Always acting all self-righteous and shit."

"I have been making the money, so for you to come at me about whether or not I'm fuckin' someone is insane. Especially when you've been eating more pussy than me and playing victim. Please miss me with all that bullshit, Indya. Look, I need to run, but I'm gonna holla at you later," he told her.

"Don't even bother!" she shouted, disconnecting the call.

He wasn't trying to be harsh by no means, but she was always going over the top and constantly playing the victim card. It was draining to the soul, which was something he didn't have time for...

CHAPTER NINETEEN

Indya hadn't accepted Deion's calls in a few days, so he had to go through her mother to check on Gianna. He knew that when she blocked him on social media she was pretty much done with him, and for the most part he felt like that was all for the best. He had no problem with giving her the space she needed to heal, but she would have to see him again because of their daughter.

"Hello," Pamela answered the phone out of breath.

"Oh, did I catch you at a bad time?" he inquired.

"No, me and Gianna been running around the house playing. "What's going on?"

"Nothing, I just wanted to check on her and see if she needed anything. Indya still isn't taking my calls."

"I'm sure she hasn't, Deion. You messed up this time. I've tried talking to her, but you know how she is when she has her mind made up. There ain't no changing it."

"Trust me, I know that all too well. Give her a kiss for me please."

"I sure will, and Deion?"

"Yes ma'am?"

"Don't stress about it too much. One thing I know about my

daughter is that she loves the ground you walk on. She'll come around," she told him.

"I know she does too. Well, I'm going to get off here. I'll Facetime you later so I can see my baby's face."

"Okay son-son, take care," she replied, hanging up before he could reply.

"Damn, who you been in there cup caking with?" Rocky asked him with a smirk.

"You funny, man. That was my daughter's grandmother," Deion replied.

"Get out that man's business," Philly replied. "You need to get some business of your own."

"I know you not talking fool," he barked.

"Y'all cut that shit out, G," Legend spoke, walking into the game room.

"This nigga always got something smart to say," Rocky spat.

"I swear y'all acting like an old married couple."

After they finished talking about business Rocky and Philly left the crib leaving Legend and Deion.

"What's up, let's take trip and get away. You know so we can take our mind off this reality shit. I can tell you're stressing out behind your shorty. I got a little cabin out in Aspen that I closed on about a year ago," Legend said. "Hit ya shorty and shit we can take her and her homegirl."

"Damn nigga, you ain't told me nothing about that. You got a whole lot of shit under your sleeves."

"Man, I ain't even told my baby moms about that shit either. That is going to be my home away from home type shit. She pisses me off and I'm out."

"I feel you on that for sure. Why you ain't got a spot somewhere tropical. You trying to freeze your balls off out there in all that damn snow."

"Man, I love the cold weather. You know it doesn't snow out here like that. Plus, it's just more peaceful out there. In the tropical climates it's always mad tourists. When I'm in my zone I rather be alone."

Deion shot Thyri a quick text asking her if they wanted to go out there with them. Of course, she hit him right back and told him they were down to go.

"Man, I ain't gone hold you I'm trying to go ASAP," Deion told him.

"Let me get Casha together and we can make something shake. I can't have her blowing my spot up again. I swear she always be popping up when I'm not thinking about her ass."

"Yeah bet, and I think it's time I find me my own spot out here. Nothing too flashy, just something big enough for me and my daughter you dig? Indya ain't letting up on my ass."

"Oh, say less. I'll hit my realtor up right now. I know he can find you something sufficient, and we don't do small around here. You're stacked with the bread why not live comfortably?"

Deion didn't bother giving Legend a fight because he knew that it would be a fight that he wouldn't win.

Whatever she had going on with the Lamika chic would need to be handled expeditiously because one thing he didn't feel like putting up with was the drama they had going on.

The main thing that he had to concern himself with was his baby girl and he wouldn't put her in any further danger. It was bad enough that he was the cause of her mother no longer being with them, but he wouldn't dare put her in any other danger.

No matter how hard he tried he couldn't convince Indya's mother to move out there. Although it would be hard raising Gianna alone, he would have to suck it up because there was nothing left in Detroit for him.

When Legend walked back in the living room, he let Deion know that his relator had a few houses on his side of town that was available to look at right away.

"Damn bruh, that was fast as hell," Deion spoke. "I barely just told your ass."

"You should know by now that I get this shit done. I ain't got nobody on my team that doesn't move at my pace. I like to get shit done. So, what's up you trying to go check these places out right now or what?" Legend asked.

Deion felt like his back was against the wall and the last thing he wanted to do was seem ungrateful. This was a once in a lifetime chance, so he took it.

"Yeah, let's do it," he replied.

"Bet, he just shot me the first location to meet him at and it's literally down the block," Legend told him.

They left the crib and was there within five minutes.

"Damn, you were right, we could have just walked down here for real."

"Bullshit, I don't walk nowhere, bro."

"I already know that. Shit, me either," Deion replied. "This shit kind of big for me and Gianna, man. I don't think I need anything like this," he honestly spoke.

"Nigga, live a little bit. Don't you think you deserve that much! I mean shit, you are up big now ain't no more of that small money you were making before. Plus, you not far from me. I got some big things set up for us. My connect see how we been moving and I'm telling you this shit will be big! Millionaire status for you, my boy."

Deion listened to everything Legend was saying, but in the back of his mind, this didn't feel right without Indya. She had been his backbone and living so lavish without her seemed wrong on so many levels. He could just hear her in his head as he thought about it.

"Deion, don't do nothing stupid! Never put more eggs in a basket than you can carry."

"Fuck it! Let me see what this shit hitting on," he said, finally replying.

Soon as Legend's relator pulled up, they headed inside, and Deion was blown away at the marble floors

"This house is five bedrooms three bathrooms; you're close to all the shopping centers and gas burning fireplaces in four of the five bedrooms. The master bedroom has a wood burning fireplace."

"You ain't gotta be so formal. This my boy he used to live out here."

Deion was in awe. Not because he hadn't seen nice homes because Legend had a dope ass crib, but because it was all he and Indya ever talked about when the first got together.

"Now if that didn't sell you, I hope this will," Mark said as they entered the kitchen. "Lovely pool, outside bar and enough space to entertain well over fifty guests."

Deion shook his head side to side still unsure about this purchase, but he also knew his credit was A-1 and the sale of his house in Detroit would bring in a nice chuck of change. He could make it work but he also didn't want to bite off more than he could chew. Hustling wasn't something that he saw himself doing past the next five years.

"Man, you can't beat this. You need to hop on it for sure," Legend urged. "Fuck it! I got you on the down payment."

"What if I like the other spot better. This shit just seems too big for me and Gianna."

"I feel you G, but this is your house and I ain't letting you pass this shit up. You need a fresh start and a fresh start that boss you all the way up."

Legend wasn't by any means trying to force the house on his boy, but he knew that he deserved it and paying his down payment wasn't shit to him. Besides that, they would be close to one another just in case.

"Damn Legend, you should be a realtor at this point. You got a deal," he told Mark.

"Great, I'll get the paperwork started."

"Soon as I get home, I will send that over to you. It was nice doing business with you again," Legend told him shaking his hand.

"Yeah, it was a pleasure," Mark replied.

"Thanks again," Deion said.

Upon leaving the house, Legend stopped in his tracks.

"Look, I know it might not seem like it now, but you about to have a new house when we get back from this little baecation, and you will be able to live the lifestyle you always wanted. You took care of them niggas in the D, got a house, a new shorty, and your baby girl. You up, my boy."

"Yeah, you're right, man. Sometimes I just feel guilty because this is just the kind of crib I promised Indya. Feel me?"

"I feel you, G. Trust me, she will be with you forever."

Deion didn't think he would ever get over the guilt, but he was going to work on it for the sake of their daughter, if nothing else...

CHAPTER TWENTY

B efore leaving, Legend made sure that all business was squared away with Philly and Rocky. They had been working with him long enough to handle the business side of things until he got back from his trip. He lied to Casha and told her that he and Deion had to go dip out to go to the plug so she wouldn't be suspicious of anything.

Friday approached faster than any of them anticipated. Everyone was packed and ready to go except Thyri.

"Girl, I been here for an hour, and you're still not finished packing! Hurry up, our flight leaves in two hours.

"Shut up! I'm coming, heffa!" she yelled.

"Well hurry up! You act like we about to be gone for a month or something."

"Ugh, you're annoying, I swear. See, I told you I was coming," Thyri teased as she came downstairs in her best fit dressed to the T.

"No wonder it took your ass so long. You look good as fuck friend."

"You know it took forever for me to lay this bomb ass orange bust down," she said flicking her hair.

"That orange is so sexy boo. Deion about to lose his mind when he sees that shit."

"Girl, I spent a nice little penny on this one "42" with the middle part. Yours look good too. What's that 30" babe?"

"Hell yeah. You know we can't go up to Aspen looking like we do any other day. We gotta give their ass a bit of exotic," Kamari replied with a giggle.

"Roll something before we get in the air boo," Thyri told her tossing her a bag of some Za.

"You're late friend. I already got this shit rolled. What you know about that? When in doubt count on me to have that shit ready."

"I just know I'm ready to go see this pretty ass snow," she replied. "I hate that we don't be getting no real snow, and soon as we get an inch the whole city shuts down."

"Me too but damn why couldn't they choose something tropical. Now that would have been the shit."

"Nah, I like that they didn't that is so typical girl. Get on social media right now, TopRock to be exact and I bet you 99 percent of them are on vacation at a tropical climate right now. I don't know, I'm a sucker for being different boo."

"Blah, whatever I'm trying to see them island men with their shirts off," Kamari said sparking the blunt. "Now, that's tea boo."

"You're a mess girl. I don't know it's something about cold weather that makes it more romantic."

"Your ass just wants to lay up with tall dark and handsome," she said teasing Thyri.

"I sure as hell do. That man, bae bee, he's not only fine but whew. Never mind," she said catching herself.

That was a major red flag talking about how a man handles you in bed, and don't get it twisted she knew her friend like that like that so that was the furthest thing from her mind but still. That wasn't what she was about to do.

"You ain't even got to say shit. I can tell by the way he got you glowing. I already know how he's coming." Kamari laughed. "Got

my girl all hot and bothered. Walking around skipping and shit."
She took a long hard pull on the blunt and passed it to Thyri.

"I mean, he iight," she replied laughing.

They chatted it up for a little bit before they finished their
blunt and headed to meet Deion and Legend at the airport. By the
time they arrived the guys were already there waiting by the truck
for them.

"It's about time y'all made it. I was starting to think y'all was
going to stand us up." Legend laughed.

"We not even that late, so cut it out Mr. Funny man," Thyri
huffed. "Hey bae." She winked at Deion as he walked over to get
her bags from the trunk but not before stealing a kiss.

"Y'all can't even wait until we get to Aspen," Kamari said
clowning.

They wasted no time complementing the girls on their looks.
Deion was in awe. Thyri was fine as frog hair, but he didn't expect
her to come out the crib killing it like that. She made his dick
jump.

"Shut that shit up and come here," Legend instructed. All she
could do was smile from ear to ear.

"That's right. Now look at you," Thyri teased.

"Let's make this shit shake," Deion said.

They all headed inside of the airport they went to a bar
before it was time for them to board their flight. After a few
drinks the foursome was feeling good and ready for their flight. It
wasn't a long flight, so they arrived at their destination in no
time.

Legend had a rental waiting when they arrived, and it was off
to his little cabin by the lake.

"Damn, I should have dressed warmer. I'm used to North
Carolina winters which aren't that bad," Thyri complained. "This
is crazy!"

"I knew you would be complaining with that thin ass jacket
on," Kamari told her as she bundled up stepping into the wintery
conditions. "Talking about you like the cold."

"It's all good I'm going to keep her warm," Deion interrupted.

"I just know you are," she replied.

"Don't worry about them because I got you," Legend replied slapping her ass.

"You better. Got me out here with all these white folks," Kamari huffed. "The lady in the ride share acted like she's never seen niggas before."

"Oh, and I have some fishing gear inside too so get ready because we're going to do some ice fishing," Legend said as he and Deion carried the bags inside.

"Hell nah! I'm not about to be out there freezing my nipples off for some funky ass fish," Kamari complained.

"Girl, hush. It's going to be fun," Thyri said pulling her friend by the arm so they could hang back a little bit. "Bitch this nigga is paid. Do you see this cabin? You might want to keep this one."

"Girl please this shit might be leased, but it's not even about that honestly. I'm falling for his vibe."

"So, the hell what girl. Leased or not his ass ain't broke and cool it doesn't have to be about that. The fact that he ain't broke is all that matters. Lord knows we done had our fair shot of broke niggas asking us for money every five minutes."

"Yeah, you're right I can't front but, Deion got money too."

"You know that is the last thing I care about. Like I said I'm just glad they're not broke niggas because Kane's ass wore me out with his nickel and diming ass. Anyway, just ease up a little bit boo. Let's enjoy this vacation out the Boro."

"A vacation consists of warm weather where I can walk around half naked getting a tan on a white sandy beach with the ocean. This is not that. It's pouring snow for Christ's sake."

"Shit, I'll take this over being home any day," Thyri told her. "You're so extra friend. Now let's go inside and try to enjoy ourselves."

"What y'all over there talking about?" Deion quizzed.

"Nothing nosey," Kamari quickly replied.

"It's a girl thing. You wouldn't understand boo," Thyri told him.

"Well, y'all come make yourselves comfortable," he replied.

"Yeah, we don't bite. Let me give y'all a tour of your new home for the week," Legend spoke.

"Wait, a week? I thought this was a weekend getaway?" Thyri quizzed.

"It was but if y'all are free why not enjoy this time together," Legend said.

They looked at each other and agreed before he had a chance to change his mind. Of course, they had to call their jobs and lie. Kamari got some fake positive COVID tests for them to show proof.

"This place is fuckin' nice as hell, Legend," Kamari said to him. "Not gone lie, I wasn't feeling this cold weather shit at first, but I think this will be good."

"Yeah, I like this," Thyri spoke. "I might need to get me a crib out here or something one day."

"I'm telling you, this is the move for real," Deion added.

"Just a little home away from home," Legend replied. "I get tired of being in the Boro sometimes and need a well-deserved break."

They all followed Legend around the cabin, amazed from one room to the next. The décor was perfect, and the space was exactly what they needed to enjoy a good week together...

CHAPTER TWENTY-ONE

Their trip was very relaxing and much needed. It was like they were all given a chance to reset and reevaluate their lives. Legend got closer to Kamari, which was unexpected. He liked her initially, but he didn't think he would fall for her so hard on their trip, but he did.

Kamari was feeling the love bug all in her soul. Legend had gotten her to loosen up more than before. He knew that she wasn't trying to give him all of her because of his baby's mother, but he was hoping now they could start on a new foot. He did everything to show her that it wasn't like that with Casha, but of course, she knew better, but that wasn't her relationship. It was theirs and theirs only.

They caught the first flight back home, so it was still very early when they got back to Greensboro PTI airport. Of course, they showed each other some love before parting ways. It was a bittersweet moment getting back to their lives but nonetheless, they were happy they had a safe and enjoyable getaway.

Kamari couldn't wait to express herself to Thyri once they were alone. Before then it was no time to tell her anything.

"Girl, I wasn't giving Legend the credit he deserved. He so

chill. That brother got me feeling myself. Whew, it's been too long since I felt this good."

"Oh, we could all see it beforehand you just couldn't but it's all good. I'm just glad you had a good time because you had me worried when we first got there." Thyri told her.

"Don't do that boo. Just because you and Deion's fine ass be cup caking on the phone and boo'd all up doesn't mean everyone else want to be like that."

"Yes, you do girl. Can't fool me, but do you want me to take you home or do you want to come back to my crib?" Thyri asked her.

"I'm coming over your house because we are stepping out tonight," Kamari told her.

"The hell you say girl. My ass is jetlagged. I need a day to get my life. I just want to crawl into my bed and chill."

"Okay you might be right about that. Oh well, I'm still coming to your crib. Stop me by my place so I can drop my shit off and grab some more clothes because whether you like it, we're going out tomorrow night."

"Shit, I already got what I want no need to hit the club boo."

"That doesn't mean you have to be an old lady, Thyri. Shit, them niggas stay at the club or strip club."

"Shut up girl. Ain't nobody said all that. You know what I mean so stop," she huffed. "Plus, I think they be up in there on their money shit."

"I know that, but I couldn't help myself. My friend be so sensitive sometimes," she teased.

"Haha," she mocked. "A bitch is so damaged it's ridiculous."

"You used to be damaged, but you have been working on yourself and that's all that matters babe," Kamari replied getting out the car to run inside her place.

Thyri was happy of the space she was in these days because God had dug her out the mud and showed her that he will always be there and would continue being there for her. She just needed to keep herself out of those dark days that once took over her life.

This chapter of her life would be filled with nothing but happiness, getting her kids back and loving herself before loving anyone else. Deion was just a bonus in the equation, and she hoped he felt the same.

Thyri got bored waiting for Kamari, so she grabbed her phone out the cup holder and got on her Facespace account. The first thing she noticed was that Deion had sent her a friend's request. She was reluctant at first, but she accepted it.

"Damn, what are you smiling so hard at boo?" Kamari said, hopping back into the car scaring Thyri half to death.

"Girl, what the hell," she snapped, covering her chest with her hand.

"I'm sorry, baby," Kamari apologized.

"It's cool but you know my ass got PTSD and shit. I was just in a daze," she said trying to laugh it off. "You just caught me off guard that's all."

"Yeah, I know. My bad, but what's up with the smile girl. Whatever it is got you all happy and shit?"

"Look at this shit," she said turning her phone in Kamari's direction.

"Oh wow! Yeah, friend you got that man's nose wide open as my granny used to say. You know these men be capping like they don't use social media so they don't have to add our ass."

"Girl, he got me open too, but I wasn't going to add him because I'm not too sure of the status with him and his baby's mother."

"Well, I hope you accepted his request," Kamari told her.

"I sure did. Like, no backsies nigga," Thyri replied laughing.

"You get on my nerves girl." Kamari laughed. "I want to check my page and see if Legend added me, but I don't want egg all on my grill if he didn't."

"I feel you on that, but it didn't even cross my mind man. I was shocked."

"He probably didn't and I'm fine with that. Okay I'm not for real but I wouldn't want to come in the way of his kids. You know bitches be bitter as hell. I won't be the reason she keeps his twins away from him."

"Yeah, there are tons of bitter baby mothers, but I don't think that is the case I mean we done been all over the Boro with them boo. She ain't tweaked out yet about it," Thyri told her.

"You are right boo, but you know what I mean. It's all good until that nigga taking you for trips."

"Now, you got a point." Thyri agreed as they headed over to her crib.

"Casha is that you?" Someone said to her as she was walking into her apartment. She spun around confused.

"Do I know you?" she quizzed while positioning her hand on her mace.

"That is you. It's Alisha, girl," she informed her.

"Damn girl, I don't have my contacts in, my bad. How you been?" Casha said, squinting her eyes to see her better.

"I been doing good for myself. I'm back in school, working at The Treasure Club. I be killing it too girl."

"That's good hun, and what? The last time I saw you I was big and pregnant as hell. My girls are four now," she told her.

"That's what's up honey. Are you still with Legend?" she inquired being nosey. Alisha knew the answer she just really wanted more information on Deion since he had been ghosting her and he hadn't been to the club in a while.

"Not really, but you know how that goes girl," she said laughing. "One minute we are and the next minute we're at each other's throat."

"Aye, what's up with his friend? We hooked up but he been MIA ever since."

"Who Deion?" she replied rolling her eyes. "He alright, I guess. I haven't been around him except if I go over Legend's crib."

"He got a girl or something?"

"That I don't know but I pulled up on Legend one morning at they had these bitches over there with them that had clearly spent the night. So, I don't know what they got going on though," she honestly spoke.

"Well, I don't do that ghosting me shit. He could have just kept it a bean with me for real."

"I feel you girl but let me go it was good seeing you. Give me your number and we can catch up later. I need to get in here and relieve my babysitter," Casha told her annoyed to no end. The last thing she wanted to think about was the next bitch her baby daddy was fucking.

"Bet, say less. Maybe you can come to the club for drinks or something," Alisha said.

"That sounds like a plan." They exchanged numbers and parted ways.

Casha didn't have any plans on kicking it with Alisha like that. She was cool and a vibe and they could go for drinks or something when she needed a break from the twins, but that would be about it because she didn't have no time to be making new friends...

Chapter Twenty-Two

Thyri was still tired from their trip, but she got up and called her job as she was scheduled to work that Friday afternoon. Since she had gotten a call back from the original appraiser about the ring, she knew her payday was about to happen, and she was going to go into business for herself. There was no way in hell that she was going to blow through the money. Texas Roadhouse would just be a thing of the past. Of course, she planned on keeping her job at the hospital because it was in her field of work, but if it came down to it, she would quit that job also. She had been doing a lot of research on being a hair vendor.

She pulled herself from her bed and headed to the shower. As the water covered her face, she breathed a sigh of relief.

After she showered and got dressed, she smoked her a blunt. Thyri was careful not to wake Kamari up when she snuck out to head over to the appraiser. She kept her fingers crossed that they would give her the original amount she had seen on the paper.

By the time Thyri made it to their location she was faded. She took a long drink of her water, poured a little bit in her hand, and splashed her face.

"Whew, get it together, bitch!" she told herself.

She walked inside and the owner greeted her right away. "Welcome, is there anything I can help you with?" she asked with a strong Russian accent. "My name is Svetlana."

"Yes ma'am. My name is Thyri Jacobs and I..." she stammered.

"Yes, Ms. Jacobs. I remember you. Now how can I help you?" she said, cutting her off.

"Um, yeah, just like I said over the phone, my boyfriend, my ex-boyfriend, came here about a year or so ago and you appraised this ring for him. I wanted to know if this amount is still good and if you're interested in buying it from me," she explained. She didn't know why she was so nervous, but her heart was in her stomach.

"Okay, let me have a look, honey," she replied, reaching her hand out.

Thyri grabbed the ring and old appraisal papers out of her purse and passed them to her. She patiently waited for her to tell her some good news. Her nerves were all over the place. She wanted to bite off her acrylic nails.

"Okay, as I look, I think I can get you at least 1.2 million," Svetlana spoke after about ten minutes of making her wait while she searched on her computer.

"What about the original amount you offered?" Thyri quizzed with a raised brow. She knew that there was a chance that she wouldn't get the same price, but she still hoped that she could get closer.

"Well, see it is the price that I gave him, but the price values drop each year, deary. Do we have a deal?" she asked with an attitude.

Thyri was disappointed but she would get over it this offer was just as good as the first one and she could come up either way.

"We have ourselves a deal," she told her as she extended her hand to shake Svetlana's.

"Great! Let me get you a cashier's check. Would you like a drink? I love to have a drink when I make such a great deal," Svetlana said as she disappeared to the back.

"Yes, I would love a drink," Thyri replied. She shot a quick text to Deion asking if he and Legend wanted to hit up Club Chaos later. She was so ready for a turnup. This was indeed the celebration she needed.

Of course, Deion texted her back right away agreeing to come. In no time Svetlana had come from the back with both her drink and her cashier's check.

"Here you go Ms. Jacobs. I hope everything is to your liking," she spoke.

"I couldn't be any better. You have no idea how idea what you've done for me," she replied throwing her drink back choking a little bit.

"That is the strongest Russian vodka young lady. You can't drink that as fast," she said with a slight chuckle. "It is meant to be sipped."

"Whew, I can tell. That's the strongest thing I've ever tasted," she replied wiping her mouth. "Thank you for everything. You take care." She was thankful but she was too excited to sit and chat with her any further.

Thyri couldn't contain herself once she got inside her car. She started screaming and crying at the same time. Her heart raced with both anticipation of cashing the check and telling Kamari.

'God, I thank you so much for this newfound wealth. I know I may not be deserving of it, but all thanks go to you.'

Thyri blasted some music and headed back home in amazing spirits. When she got back to the house Kamari was up cooking breakfast.

"Girl where the hell were you at? I was blowing your shit up," she said coming out the kitchen when she heard Thyri come inside.

"Remember that ring?"

"Yeah, were you able to sell it?"

"Hell yes! Look at this," Thyri said excitingly as she pulled the check from her bag.

"Is this shit real? Wow! This is crazy! You're fuckin' rich," Kamari said holding her chest.

"Yesss it's real as hell girl!! I'm so happy! Now all I got to do is get my kids back and my life will be complete," she said as tears of joy poured from her eyes. I had to bring this shit home before even going to the bank. Oh, and we are most definitely Club Chaos later. I already asked Deion and they're down."

"Nah, I think this is a strip club kind of night. I want to spend some money."

"Girl, you really think them niggas are going to be down to chill with us in the strip club that's like taking sand to the beach," Thyri said to her.

"I mean if not then we can go, but I'm not looking forward to seeing that whore ass foster sister of yours. They can party some-where else. And shit, they met us in the damn strip club, or did you forget?"

"No bitch! I'm trying to kick it with my bestie and new bae, and true they did but it's different," Thyri said dancing around the living room wearing a wide smile. "As for Alisha, we can just go to another club boo."

"Nah, we're going to her job because I want to see that shit for myself or if that's another one of her lies."

"Honestly, I don't care either way. I'm just wanting to enjoy my people. She added me on Facespace but she hasn't sent me any messages. She did love the pictures from our trip though."

"Is there a particular reason why you ain't tell me about that? You tell me everything Thyri. I'm team not Alisha and never will be. That girl is trouble, and you know I'm right. She's always on bullshit."

"Ugh, I know but we are not about to ruin the good vibes behind her ass I have too much to be happy about. Now cheer up let's eat and drink bookie. Since you cooked, I'll make us some Mimosas," Thyri told her.

She didn't care what Kamari was saying about Alisha there

was too much to be thankful for. This would not be the negative vibes to kill her good vibrations.

They ended up meeting the guys because Thyri wanted to drive her own ride this time so she could leave on her own. She hated being on anyone else's time especially when it came to going out.

Thyri and Kamari both wore Amiri long sleeve track suits. Thyri's was beige with black lettering and Kamari's was black with beige lettering and they both wore Ugg's. It was cold and they didn't have anyone to impress so track suits it was.

They ended up getting to the club before Legend and Deion. Thyri was trying her best to understand why Deion was so dry when she told him where they were meeting. It was just the shift in his energy that she picked up on.

"Girl, maybe he gave that reaction because you changed plans last minute. I'm sure it's nothing. Relax boo I'm sure it's nothing. We're going to have a good time."

"If you say so girl," Thyri replied as they walked into The Treasure Club.

"Anyway, are we getting a section or what?" Kamari asked her.

"Hell yeah, this is a major celebration, so VIP it is!"

Thyri paid for their section and Kamari paid for a couple of bottles and some hot wings. Soon as the vibes started, they saw their men coming through the doors.

"Look," Kamari told Thyri. She stopped throwing money on the big booty girl that was in their section shaking her ass. The second that she met eyes with Deion her day became better somehow. To her this was her man. I don't know, I guess you know when it's real.

"Hey baby," she greeted him wrapping her arms around his neck kissing his cheek when he made it to her.

"What's good baby," he replied. "Come here," he said leading her closer to the door. Reluctantly she went. Of course, she wondered why he was pulling her to the side.

"You good? Why you bring me all the way over here?" she quizzed looking around.

"Oh, it's not nothing for real. I just wanted to let you know that I only didn't want to come here because I ain't never had a shorty that wanted to be around me in a strip club this is some new shit for me for real," he lied.

"Say what?" she asked. "I couldn't hear you." She danced around while repeated what he had said.

"You came and that's all that matters baby. I guess I understand, but if you haven't noticed it yet, I'm different," Thyri told him with a wink. "Now can we go enjoy this ass and our friends."

Deion just smiled and followed her back to their section. As he surveyed the club, he didn't see Tasty anywhere. He quickly breathed a sigh of relief. She was the last face he wanted to see in there.

"It's about time your asses came back. This is not a baecation if y'all haven't noticed," Kamari said laughing.

"Shut up smart ass!" Thyri yelled over the music.

"So, now that all of that is done can we take some shots!" Legend shouted.

They all threw their shots back and partied. Thyri flagged over a few dancers to their section to show Legend and Deion a good time.

"Now this is what I call a motherfuckin' party!" Legend said slapping Kamari's ass. "We got some true bitches!"

"Nigga watch your fuckin' mouth! Ain't neither of us bitches!" Kamari spat.

"Chill boo, it's all good," Thyri told her grabbing her into a hug.

"What's the celebration about!?" Deion asked shouting over the music.

"I promise to tell you all about it tomorrow, babe," Thyri replied. "Let's just soak all of this up." She was feeling herself.

She watched as they all enjoyed themselves. This is what life was all about. Watching the people, you care about experiencing life together. Just as quickly as things were good, they weren't.

Thyri rolled her eyes soon as she saw Alisha come out from the back of the club and head for their section. She knew that Kamari was sauced up enough to put hands on Alisha if she came out her mouth with some slick shit, but Thyri was going to do her best to defuse it if it came to that.

"Thyri, hey my baby! What's up boo," Alisha said as she smiled at everyone.

"Bye Alisha! You ain't fuckin' our night up," Kamari gritted.

Legend looked over to Deion and he was more nervous than a hooker at church. "Go shake that funky shit somewhere else because we're good over here!"

"Ugh, you're miserable," she mumbled as she turned her attention to Deion and Legend.

"Hey girl. You look so pretty," Thyri complimented. "This club be jumping! I know your money be right!" Thyri was doing everything she could to keep the peace.

"Thank you! Hey Deion," she said giving him that look of seduction you give someone you've fucked before.

"You see that shit," Kamari slurred loudly over the music. Thyri had tunnel vision as she glared at Deion's response.

"Sup," he replied turning back to Legend trying to ignore her. Little did he know that she was only in their faces to start some shit because she was just miserable like that.

"This is some shit right here. I knew we shouldn't have come here!" Legend barked when he saw Casha blow right past the door and make a beeline to their section.

"What was that about Deion," Thyri snapped.

"Man, it ain't shit for real," he told her as the music paused in the background.

"Damn, and here I thought we had something. Sorry sis, but this nigga knows what it is," Alisha spoke cockily.

Thyri just looked at Deion and shook her head. "Let's go! I'm over this bullshit!"

"Fuck that! We're not going anywhere!" Kamari cursed. "That whore ain't about to run us off!"

"Oh, so you on this bitch like that?!" Casha snapped as she invaded their section.

"You been fuckin' with her?" Thyri grilled. The tension was bouncing off the walls like ping-pong balls.

"It's not what you think," he started but was interrupted by Casha charging at Kamari.

Alisha was the type to throw rocks and hid her hands, so she took a step back because she knew she couldn't fight, and she couldn't afford to lose her job.

"Beat that bitch's ass!" Thyri yelled. By this time, they had the attention of all the patrons of the club. She wanted to be peaceful, but these hoes weren't about to let that happen, so she with all the bullshit.

Legend jumped up and snatched Casha up before security made it to them.

"Yo, what the fuck are you on?" he spazzed. "We ain't shit!"

"Because, nigga! You out here taking this bitch on trips and shit while me and your kids ain't seen shit! Fuck outta here!" she spat. He was lost for words because Rocky and Philly were the only two that knew where he was going.

"I'm good on this shit," Thyri spoke, doing her best to drag Kamari out the club. There was no way in hell that she was about to catch a case over this bullshit.

"Aye, this ain't the place to be on that ghetto hoodrat shit!" the DJ said. "Kick they asses out and let's get our girl Tasty to the stage."

"Come on, let me help you," Deion told her as he tried escorting them out the club.

"Nah, I got this! You go handle that bitch!" Thyri cut. "I'm good on your ass too! Leave me the fuck alone!"

When they finally made it to the car, Thyri busted out crying.

She couldn't hold it in any longer. That shit really hurt her feelings to the core.

"I didn't sign up for none of this shit! I guess I know why his punk ass didn't want to come out here. I should have known it was something because we met up in that bitch."

"It's okay boo, I beat that hoe ass too!" Kamari slurred.

"It ain't even about that shit, man," she huffed. "Alisha can have his ass!"

"So, beating her ass will make you feel better," Kamari cursed as she pulled her phone from her bra to call Legend.

Thyri sighed heavily and dried her tears. This was the last thing she needed in her life. Today was supposed to be a fresh new chapter in her life. Her night wasn't supposed to end like that at all. Her heart was hurting. It didn't matter how young she was. She was tired of getting her heart broken...

CHAPTER TWENTY-THREE

Kamari woke up puking her guts out. Thyri stood behind her and held her hair, contemplating her next steps. She still couldn't wrap her mind around what had happened the night before. It wasn't that she cared what Deion had done before her, but the fact that he hadn't told her anything. He had to know they would run into each other. I mean, fuckin' a stripper prior to their link was blowing her, and let's be honest. The fact that it was Alisha made the situation that much more intolerable.

"Oh, what the fuck, girl!" Thyri yelled as her friend tried coming up for air but only spewed puke that splashed all over her feet.

"I'm so sorry." Kamari winced in pain as she began dry heaving over and over.

"I'm never letting you get that drunk again," Thyri warned.

"Shut up, you would have been torn down too but niggas blew your shit." Kamari sat up and went to the sink to wash her face and brush her teeth.

"I guess you're right, but that nigga could have just kept it a buck with me. It's not like I'm his girl or some shit. All he had to say was that he smashed one of the dancers and I wouldn't have even pressed him about coming there. That shit was embarrassing as fuck."

"You know damn well a nigga not gone tell you about who he done fucked, girl. I get it because I'd be livid too. I fuckin' told you not to fuck with that hoe Alisha! Chances are she knew he was messing with you and decided to come and fuck up what y'all had going on."

"As badly as I would like to be mad at you, I can't because you were right. I probably wouldn't have been as mad, but she basically acted like she wanted to reconnect with me, and you know how much I cared for her. She preyed on that and played in my face. It's all good though, she can have his ass," she spat. "I'm not fighting a literal pass-around ass bitch behind NO NIGGA!"

"Fuck out of here! You are not about to cut him off over her, Thyri. I know you're pissed, but that is basically telling her you're not only bothered but that you're also giving up. You're basically pushing them into each other's arms at this point, girl."

Just then Thyri's phone started ringing and she quickly disconnected the call once she saw that it was Deion calling. He had been calling her nonstop.

"I don't have shit to say to that man for real, and ain't nobody giving up! Do you know how dumb that shit made me feel? He could have spared me, but he didn't," she huffed. "He let me sit there with egg on my face. Nah, I'm good."

"Come on, Thyri. You can't shut down and shut that man out like that. At least give him a chance to explain himself."

"Whatever, give me fifteen. I'm about to take a shower, heffa," Thyri said, trying to shoo her friend out of the bathroom so she could think with a clear mind and with no distractions.

"Girl, the shower is over there. You can get in all you want. You ain't about to dodge this conversation. You know damn well I'm not looking at ya ass!"

"You're so fuckin' annoying, Kamari," she huffed as she stepped behind the wall to get undressed.

"Call it what you want boo, but you can't diss that good ass man behind Alisha's ass."

"He is a good man Savannah, head ass! Spare me, Kamari."

Thyri was so not trying to have that conversation, but she was trapped. She wasn't hearing nothing Kamari was saying.

"You know how I feel about lying ass people. That shit grinds my gears. Do whatever but lying is just as bad as being a damn thief and neither are to be trusted."

"Shit, who doesn't hate a liar but technically he didn't have to tell you because that was before you friend."

"Omission is still a fuckin' lie Kamari!" She spat as she stepped into the steaming hot shower. "Oh shit! This too hot!"

"Thyri, y'all been kicking it for a few months and although shit wasn't etched in stone. Y'all might as well had been together. And let's not start on that Omission shit! I know damn well you ain't told him half of what you been through," Kamari told her.

"No, I haven't, because we're not like that. I mean, I hoped that we would be, and of course I would have mentioned it," she replied. "I don't care how much I'm feeling that nigga. Shit, if I told him a fraction of the shit I've been through he would dip out so fast my head would spin around fast as Linda Blair's in *The Exorcist*."

"I totally get it but like I said, give him the opportunity to tell his side of things. I mean, it's apparent that y'all really care for each other." Soon as the words came out her mouth she began coughing.

"Better watch how you're coughing because you're about to be throwing up again," Thyri spoke, but was too late. Kamari was hugging the toilet again.

"Fuck! Yeah, I'm never getting that drunk again. I know it was because I was mixing," she huffed, wiping her mouth.

"You always say that shit, girl. You'll be just fine soon as it's out of your system. Now get out so I can hop out."

Kamari quickly splashed her face and rinsed her mouth out before she left the bathroom.

Thyri got out the shower, wrapped the large towel around her body. She stepped to the mirror and wiped the steam off. She took a very long and observing look at herself. *'You got this baby.'*

She really was feeling Deion and everything about him, but she wasn't about to let him think that lying to her would ever fly in her book. I mean it wasn't the ultimate betrayal so she could and would eventually forgive him for not telling her about Alisha. It just made what they had feel less special knowing that he had smashed a stripper but hell she had to also be honest with herself because she was sure most men smashed strippers especially if given the chance.

Thyri got seven follow up calls from Deion along with several text messages all of which she ignored and powered her phone off.

"Girl, I wish you would take his calls because every time you ignore him Legend is blowing me up. Shit, I don't even want to talk to him because unlike Deion he is still very much fuckin' with his crazy ass baby mother. That's something that I'm not going to deal with. He needs to get his shit together."

"Look how the tables turned that quick. We just knew we had had two good ass niggas and they're just as rotten as the rest of the bunch. I don't know Kam I just don't want to put any energy into nothing that doesn't add value to my life."

"Deion does add value girl. Do you know what you have overcome? I'm sorry but I gotta give that man his props because you were a mess before you got with him."

"You have a point, I was a mess, but that don't mean that I want to deal with bullshit either, Kamari," she huffed. "I don' t know, I just guess I wasn't expecting this either. Ugh, never mind man, you're not getting it," she huffed, annoyed. Kamari was pissing her off acting like she wouldn't be pissed off too. There was no way in hell that she thought what Deion had done was okay.

Thyri knew that Kamari cared for her so her feelings were likely valid, because the way she pushed her and Deion's relationship was almost like she feared that Thyri would spin the block on Kane whenever he was released.

"I'm sorry if I'm being pushy, but I have never seen you so happy, girl. You were in a bad place not too long ago that I didn't think you would ever overcome, but you did, and I believe that Deion is the reason for that."

"You don't have to apologize, Kam. Maybe I'm being a brat about it. I just don't like the thought of bumping heads once again with Alisha's ass."

"That probably wasn't by accident. I have been telling you ever since she popped back up to not deal with her, girl. Just because you have a soft spot for her means nothing to a bum bitch like her. I hate that you had to go through this again, but please block her from your page and don't look back. I'm telling you right now, like it or not, I'm going to fuck her up if she tries any more slick shit. I been waiting on her ass," Kamari warned.

"I'm sure she did that shit intentionally, but it's all good. Trust me, you don't have to worry about laying hands on her because I'm going to teach her ass a lesson once and for all for playing with me. She done had too many chances and I was still willing to give her the benefit of the doubt. And I blocked her as soon as we got to the crib last night. I'm good on her."

Thyri's ego was bruised because not only did Deion play in her face, but Alisha had also. If they knew what was good for them, they would leave her alone and stay far away from her...

CHAPTER TWENTY-FOUR

"You have been moping around for weeks. When are you going to go get your man back?" Mariah quizzed.

"I honestly don't know if I'm ready to get back with him. He needs to learn a lesson and miss my ass. That man has taken me through so much, and honestly, my mind is elsewhere," Indya admitted.

"Let me find out Maurice got you sprung," Mariah teased.

"No, he doesn't, girl. That man is worse than Deion's ass. But he does keep a smile on my face. I ain't giving him none though. I'll be damned if I let another man get me like I was behind Deion."

"You know damn well you're going to cave, Indya. You have been glowing ever since he came into your job and asked if you would represent him."

"He does have a certain something-something that makes me interested but girl, that man used to come to my house with Deion. That's playing with fire. That man would lose his mind if he found out that I was representing him and would probably kill both of our asses if we fucked around. I'm good on that because I love my life, girl."

"You know damn well that man ain't built like that. He tries to be a thug, but I've never met a real estate gangsta before," she clowned.

"Oh, you're real funny. Nah, but for real, I do miss Deion though."

"I know you miss him girl, he has been in your life for years. You can't just get over someone that easily. Why not just call him and tell him that?"

"Mariah, you know better than anyone that I've tried everything. I can't make him do better. I thought the threesome was going to make us solid again."

"You know I love you girl, but not all men are into that. Besides that, it was me. He was already salty that it was me that joined y'all. I'm sure that was a hard pill to swallow. You know these niggas can't take what they dish out."

"I get that and I'm not mad. My problem was that he flew his ass back up the highway and didn't bother telling me until I mentioned it."

"Listen, I'm not going to sugarcoat this shit for you. He is more than likely fuckin' with a whole different bitch out there. I know his business has been slow but for him to use every excuse to leave, he got somebody else. I say we take off work. Hell, use vacation time and go out there and find out what it is he's really doing. I got a homegirl out there that can put us in the right circle. She knows everybody," Mariah explained.

"I want to disagree with you but you're right. Of course, it came across my mind, but I was giving him a chance because he convinced me that he didn't feel right to allow me to pay all the bills since he haven't been having clients since the pandemic. You know my dumb ass fell for every word too," she replied shaking her head.

"So, what's up are we going out there or what?" Mariah probed.

"Maybe, I got to make sure that I want to know first. Why go out there if I don't care what the outcome will be. I'll let you know though."

Indya was side eyeing the hell out of Mariah because at the point she seemed more concerned about what Deion was doing more than her. For all she knew her friend was playing her close so she could be with Deion. She felt it deep in her spirit that their little rendezvous was going to be the demise of their relationship. She wanted to go pull up on him in hood rat fashion but truthfully, she didn't think she could handle another betrayal.

Deion sat on his phone looking through his and Thyri's pictures saddened. He couldn't believe shorty had blown his spot up like that. Shit how was he supposed to know they knew each other. Tasty was just a freak he got some pussy from during a rough time in his life. He had not one intention of fucking with her on that level and he didn't touch her after that. He had no idea that she was that thirsty. Her telling Thyri anything about him fucking should have never happened.

The more he tried calling Thyri the more she ignored him. Although he didn't want to fall back, she was leaving him with no choice in the matter. When he went to her pages, but he was blocked already.

Damn, I really fucked up, man, he thought.

"Nigga, what the fuck you do to lose that fine ass bitch Thyri?" Rocky said, laughing.

"First of all, little ass nigga, watch your mouth. She ain't no bitch and it's none of your fuckin' business," he barked, standing up and towering over Rocky. Deion didn't like that disrespecting women shit.

"Oh, nigga you don't want smoke with me. I'm not them hoe ass niggas you're used to!" He said as he rose to his feet. Rocky wasn't no hoe, and he was standing on big business. "I' m just saying. Nigga mad at me because his bitch dissed him!"

"Yo chill man," Legend said laughing stepping between them.

"Y'all nigga's need to put the Yack down if y'all about to be on this bullshit!"

"Nah, fuck that his short ass. He stays with the slick shit. Always with the jokes when ain't nothing funny." Deion was tired of Rocky's mouth.

"Come on Deion chill. This ain't even worth it," Philly spoke up.

"Y'all might be on this niggas sack but I'm sure the fuck not!" Rocky gritted.

"Cut that shit out Rocky, you know better than that! How you mad he don't want you calling his woman a bitch," Legend barked. "Where is all of this coming from." They were all flabbergasted because until now Rocky seemed to be cool with Deion.

"Whatever bruh I'm out!" Rocky huffed making his way to the front door with his package. "I ain't coming back over here on that type of time until he takes his ass back home."

"Mad ass nigga can suck my dick!" Deion said making him a drink. The last thing he wanted to do was beef with one of Legend's niggas, but dude was out of pocket. Deion was just waiting for all his business to be taken care of so he wouldn't have to ever cross paths with Rocky again. If anything, Legend could bring the work to his spot since it wouldn't be far from his crib. Deion was glad that he copped a little condo so he could have his own space. Indya was still on her bullshit so although he hadn't shut his business down in Charlotte yet, it wouldn't be long before he did. She was answering his calls letting him Facetime with Gianna but that was about it and he couldn't ask for more.

"Fuck that sensitive ass nigga. Let us get back to the money shit," Legend said. "Rocky just in his bag because you checked him. Trust me he will be back around with no problem. You just hit his ego."

"Damn nigga, why are you giving us so much this time?" Philly quizzed afraid he wouldn't be able to move his product as fast.

"You got this nigga and yo ass ain't never complained before now," Legend said with a suspicious look.

"Nah, man it's cool I was just asking. Shit, you know I got this," he announced. "More money for me."

Deion's phone started chiming over and over. His heart fluttered hoping it was Thyri calling him back to squash shit, but he wasn't so lucky. It was Alisha sending him a message on his social media.

"Fuck!" he shouted. "What this bitch reaching out to me for. She'll be lucky if I don't put somebody on her ass for that shit she pulled last night," he barked.

"Man, that bitch is like a blunt everybody can hit it!" Philly told him laughing.

"Shit, I was just trying to get my dick wet so to speak. "Who knew she would be acting like this?"

"Look, just block that bitch!" Legend told him.

"Nigga, you're late. Soon as I saw the message request I blocked her goofy ass," Deion replied.

"Yeah, fuck that bitch," Legend said passing him the blunt.

"Just what I need to clear my mind man."

"Well, I'm about to get up out of here. Let me know if y'all need me, let me know," Philly said dismissing himself.

As soon as he opened the door to leave, Casha and the twins came in with Alisha on her heels.

"Legend! Where you at?" Casha yelled out as she made her way through the house.

"Got damn! Here this bitch goes!" Legend barked as she finally made her way to the game room where he they spent most of their time.

"Y'all got them hoes up in here," she said looking around as she walked through the house.

"Bruh, what are you doing over here?" Deion demanded to know the second he locked eyes with Alisha.

"Damn, you don't want to see me?" she said as she approached Deion looking crazy. In her mind he was all hers when she saw Thyri and leave him standing in the middle of the club.

"Bitch, you pulled that fuck shit last night. I'm all the way good on you! The pussy was decent, but not all of that," he barked.

"Wow it's like that? I thought we had a good time though?"

"We did and when I ain't reach out that should have let you know I wasn't on that type of time," Deion replied.

"I knew I ain't like this nigga. Me and Legend was good before you brought your ass down here!"

"Shut the fuck up, Casha. What the fuck are you here for anyway? If it's not about my kids I'm done! This back a fourth is draining as fuck. How y'all know each other?" he asked puzzled because in the five years they had been together she never mentioned knowing Alisha.

"You got some fuckin' never Legend. I wasn't draining before you started smashing that bitch now, was I?" she huffed. "And don't worry about how we know each other."

"Hey, my beautiful babies," he said dismissing her as he picked up each of his daughters and planted kisses over their faces.

Deion was happy for his boy, but his soul ached for his daughter. Seeing Legend spend time with his girls made him depressed that was the how it was with Indya. The only thing that gave him solace was Thyri and now she wasn't even talking to him. He grabbed one of the bottles of Hennessey from behind the bar.

"Aye bruh, I'm about to go up to my room let me know if you need me," he told Legend.

"Damn nigga, you dippin' out on me like that?" he asked hoping he sounded sad enough for him to stay downstairs. Lord only knew he didn't want to be left with Casha nor Alisha's janky ass.

"Damn, you're rude as fuck! I came here to see your ass," Alisha spat.

Deion ignored her went to his room, rolled a fat ass blunt and started taking shots. He had given up now on calling Thyri. He needed to hear Gianna's voice. It never mattered what he was dealing with her calling him daddy made his day better.

"Hi daddy," she greeted when he called.

"Hey princess bear," he replied with a wide smile. He couldn't believe Pamela had let her answer his call. "Daddy misses you so much."

"Okay daddy."

"I love you, baby." Her face was just that of her mother's. He tried smiling through the tears.

"Love you."

"Give your Mimi the phone," he told her.

"I'm right here," she said, taking the phone from Gianna. "Is everything okay with you, son? You look sad?"

"I will be okay. How has Indya been? She's still pissed with me."

"She is just fine, working like crazy, but she's okay."

"Well, let her know that I asked about her," he replied.

"I gotcha, take care."

"You too, peace."

Deion felt a lot better after hearing Gianna's little voice. He needed a plan on how to get back in Thyri's good graces. He hated that they ended the way they had...

CHAPTER TWENTY-FIVE

Over the next month, Thyri's life had completely changed for the better. Of course, she hadn't reconciled with Deion, but that didn't stop him from trying to reach out every chance he got. Once her check cleared at the bank, she couldn't wait to buy a house in Hidden Oaks. The homes in that area were expensive but not too much to break her pockets. She also brought her a small window front office space to open her hair shop where she would sell human hair, lace fronts, and other little trinkets for hair. The space would also include a chair where you could get slayed after getting your hair if you wanted to.

Thyri still needed to get a bomb-ass hairdresser and finish setting up for the grand opening. It was a little bit overwhelming, but she had Kamari to help her with everything. She was taking classes so she could learn how to do lashes. Thyri wanted her spot to be a one-stop shop. Envy Hair Haven.

Having the ability to make life better gave Thyri a sense of completion. Within the last week, she had been granted visitation to see her kids. The ball was moving in the right direction for her to get her kids back and she couldn't be happier if she tried to. She had her shop about to open and she and Kamari were looking better than ever. Yes, her love life was suffering, but she was just fine.

Her worker Samantha let her know that since she had the means to take care of her kids, she would have them within the next six months if she kept up the good work. That's all Thyri needed to hear because she had no intentions of messing this up. Knowing she was going to get her kids back was all the motivation she needed to keep pushing.

As for her oldest daughter she was with a foster family that didn't want to be bothered with trying to reunite them. However good for Thyri that she didn't lose her under crazy circumstances so they would have to file the proper paperwork to make it happen. She would of course keep her fingers crossed and prayers up high.

Thyri posted on her Facespace account talking about happy she was that her life would be complete soon. There was an outpouring amount of support for her because the people in her hometown knew that she never deserved to lose them anyway.

Alisha had made page after page trying to get her attention enough to apologize to her for what she had done but Thyri wasn't having it she just blocked any account she messaged her from and kept it moving. Thyri was not about to let her play in her face again.

Thyri needed to go to the beauty supply store to get some more lace glue so she could lay her hair down. She didn't want to go alone so she called Kamari.

"Hello," she answered.

"Hey boo, are you busy?"

"Hell no, but I was headed your way," Kamari told her.

"Bet." She giggled. "I was calling to see if you felt like running to the beauty shop on Bessemer. I need to go there and a few more spots and you know I hate going out alone."

"Cool I'm about to pull up in about five minutes."

"So, ten minutes then. Cool."

"Oh nah, I'm not on CP time." She laughed.

"Good, and I have something for you too," Thyri told her.

"What is it?"

"You'll see when you get here friend."

"Ugh, whatever," she huffed.

"Later girl," she said disconnecting the call.

Thyri made sure all her lights in the house was off and everything was locked up before Kamari pulled up. Soon after she heard a horn beep and she set the alarm on her house and headed outside.

"Look at my rich friend. Got me coming over to this white neighborhood and shit," Kamari teased.

"Girl bye, I'm going to forever be Thyri. I just had to leave the hood." She giggled as she got into the car. "I'm just glad Kane can't find my ass."

"Why in the hell we not rolling in your new Benz boo? I knew for sure you would want to floss your shit."

"Come on you know me better than that girl. It's just a car, but here," Thyri said passing her an envelope with a customized thank you card inside.

'Kamari, where do I even begin. We have been through so much together. I love you more than any words can express. My life wouldn't be what it is today if you weren't here with me, pushing me, praying with me, loving me. It's nothing in this world I wouldn't do for you, my baby.'

Love Always, Thyri

Tears of joy poured down her thick cheeks. "I love you so much more, baby," she said, giving her a hug.

"Stop that crying shit before you have my crybaby ass in here crying too, but there is more," she told her as she passed her a cashier's check for fifty thousand dollars.

"Oh shit! Thyri, stop playing with me! Are you fuckin' serious right now?!" she said as she bounced around in the driver's seat. Thyri looked at her friend and she could no longer fight the waterworks off. Big heavy tears trundled down her face.

"You think that is good enough boo?"

"Fuck yeah!" she replied drying her face. "You know you didn't have to do this right?"

"Hush, I know that. I wanted to do that for you. You deserve to be happy too."

"Saying thank you doesn't seem like enough, but thank you so much, girl." She hugged her again and this time she refused to let go. They held one another for at least five more minutes before breaking free.

"Just seeing your reaction is priceless. No need to say thank you my love I know you appreciate it and that is all that matters," Thyri honestly spoke.

"Come on you know we're going to have to go out so I can celebrate. I mean since you ain't been wanting to go out with me," Kamari said as they hopped on West Market. "I'm putting this bitch in my titty until I get to the bank."

"I love you girl, but I'm trying to get my head together. I don't want to even entertain people right now."

"Look I know you been in your little funk since Deion but this ain't about nobody but us. You need to stop being mean to that man he loves you."

"Aht, aht, don't give me that. Your ass was mad at Legend too. Don't be trying to push me off on him since y'all niggas back cool," she huffed.

"It's not that boo but anyone with eyes could see that y'all brought out the best in each other. All I'm saying is I think you should at least hear him out. You're all he talks about, and I know he loves you. The way that man's face lights up when your name is mentioned or even when he brings you up is unmatched," she explained.

Thyri was listening to everything Kamari had to say, and she still had it bad for him, but facts were facts, and he had fucked her foster sister and that was a hard pill to swallow.

"I hear you girl. Who knows we'll see what happens but right now getting my kids has my attention."

"As it should be. Just call him or we can cook and shit, invite them over to your new house. You know a small housewarming," Kamari said as she pulled into the parking lot of the beauty supply store.

"Yeah, I said I hear you. Come on, are you coming in here or you are you going to stay in the car. I'm just grabbing some lip gloss and lace glue so I can lay my shit. I didn't want to come but some of my orders are still in transit." Thyri stepped out the car.

"Yeah, I need to grab some shit too for real."

They went inside and basically looked around at some of their prices because Thyri was either online or going around checking prices, she wanted to have the cheapest prices in town when her shop opened.

By the time Thyri was checking out Kamari was just making it to the register with two hands full of shit.

"Give me the keys," Thyri told her. "I'm about to go spark this blunt in bag."

"Ugh, just wait it won't take them but a second to ring me up girl."

"No heffa, I'm trying to hit my blunt," she told her heading out the door. It seemed like soon as she walked out Kamari heard rapid gun fire. She tried bolting out the door, but an older woman slung her to the floor.

"Let me fuckin' go, my friend is out there!" she yelled, kicking and screaming trying to break away from the woman's tight grip.

Soon as the gunfire stopped, the woman let her go and Kamari bolted out the door. She was met with a sight she could have gone a lifetime without seeing. Thyri was sprawled out on the ground with a gunshot to the right shoulder.

"Who the fuck did this?" Kamari cried as she pressed her hand tightly on Thyri's shoulder.

"I, I—Lamika," Thyri stammered in a whisper. Thyri was trying her best to breathe but she was starting to get cold. Her body was quivering, and her hands were wet and clammy. She didn't know if she was dying or in shock.

"Stop standing around and call the fuckin' ambulance!"

Kamari shouted. "It's going to be okay, baby. Please stay with me, boo." She looked over and noticed that she was still gripping her Glock. Kamari quickly grabbed it from her and tucked it into her jeans so the police wouldn't ask any questions. She didn't care if Thyri was licensed to carry or not. She ain't have time for the unnecessary questions. There was so much blood she didn't know where blood was coming from.

Thyri gripped her hand and glared into her eyes and mumbled, "I love you."

"You're going to be alright, baby. Just stay with me, please," Kamari pleaded. "Bet you're glad you ain't drive that Benz, huh?"

Thyri cracked a smile and closed her eyes just as Kamari heard the ambulance nearing...

CHAPTER TWENTY-SIX

K
amari paced the floor, biting her fingernails, a nervous wreck waiting on the nurse or doctor to get back with her after they took Thyri back for emergency surgery. Her mind was racing, and she couldn't think straight to save her life. At that moment, she didn't know whether Thyri's injuries were life-threatening, but hearing that she needed surgery scared her to no end.

Finally sitting down to try and calm herself, she scrolled social media trying to take her mind off everything, and her phone started ringing. It was Legend. He was calling to see if she got Thyri to agree to see Deion. Her mind was so gone that she forgot all about calling and telling them what had happened.

"Hello," she answered out of breath.

"Yo shorty, you good? What's wrong?" he quizzed, wondering why she sounded the way she did.

"No," she cried. "Thyri just got shot and she's in surgery."

"What! We on the way man where y'all at?"

"Moses Cone," she replied trying to stop herself from crying to no avail.

"Bet give us fifteen and we'll be there for sure," he told her disconnecting the call. "Don't cry shorty we on the way."

Legend ran up the stairs taking them two by two so he could let Deion know what had happened.

"Yo nigga, wake up!" he yelled barging up into his bedroom completely forgetting that Deion had moved into his crib a week prior.

"Fuck!" Legend bolted out the door hopped in his whip. He damn near left his car in drive he was such in a rush to let him know what happened. He rang the doorbell over and over until Deion came to the door groggy.

"What the fuck man!" He shouted. Deion was in the middle of a dream.

"Let's go! We gotta get to the hospital! Thyri just got shot. Kamari said she's in surgery right now."

His heart sank, this déjà vu had him back at a place he never wanted to revisit for a long as he lived. Deion sat there for a few minutes trying to take it all in, but none of it made any sense until he went back to the day he had went to her crib and shorty had flamed at her crib.

"Nigga! You hear me? Get up let's go!" Legend barked snapping his fingers at him.

"Yeah, yeah I'm coming," he dryly replied still trying to wrap his mind about this news.

He was so thrown off he forgot to put pants on. When they made it to the hospital is when he realized that he only had basketball shorts on.

"Damn man, I done forgot my damn pants. Fuck it let's go see if Kamari got any word yet," he said exciting the SUV.

They rushed inside and hurried to the emergency department. Deion was walking like his ass was on fire leaving Legend behind. They ended up running into Kamari at the coffee machine. She desperately needed a drink, but coffee would have to suffice.

"Aye, what happened?" Deion said from behind her scaring her half to death.

"Hey y'all. The doctor just came, and they have her in a medically induced coma just to speed up the healing process.

They're saying her chances are good for the most part. She was shot in the right shoulder and grazed in her hip."

"Who the fuck did this shit?" Legend asked with a raised brow.

"Was it the same bitch that shot at her crib that day?" Deion quizzed. "I knew she should have handled that shit!"

"Yeah, it was that bitch, Lamika that's what Thyri said just before she blacked out. I got Thyri's gun though, but I didn't think to see if she had fired it for real. I just wanted to make sure the cops didn't find it in case she hit her.

"Where she be at?" Deion barked. He was ready to go hunt her down and make sure she paid for what she had done.

"Yeah, we'll take that bitch down for sure. Fuck that!" Legend spoke.

"Look can we worry about her ass another day. We need to focus on Thyri. The doctor said there wasn't anything life threatening so I'm sure she will be alright. My nerves are just shot.

"Well, if 12 ain't been here yet they're on the way," Legend told her. "Trust me they will know what is going on and they will be here wanting answers."

"I hope so because I ain't about to tell the nothing. We will handle that bitch ourselves," Kamari cried laying on Legends chest. "Why would she do this man."

"It's gone be okay baby. Y'all don't know why she did that shit? I mean I know this is a hard ass time for you, but she couldn't have done it for no reason."

Kamari led them to the waiting area and although she did not want to out her friend there wasn't a better time to let them know why they were all there. After they were seated, she just blurted it out. Of course, not telling too much.

"Alright, so Thyri's ex Kane is very sick in the head and delusional which is why his ass is locked up now," she began.

"Just take your time. I mean don't tell us all her business, but just let us in a little bit," Deion told her. "Lord knows I don't want her mad at me more than what she already is right now."

"Yeah, I know. Anyway, he was very possessive and shit. He used to watch her location and everything. He jumped on her real bad sending her to the hospital and after that she got a restraining order on him. Months later we out clubbing see him with another broad and everything," she explained and continued with her story. "Thyri was happy for real, so she linked with one of her ex's Lamar and the next day when he was taking her home Kane beat that man within an inch of his life. He is Lamika's twin brother, and she blames Thyri for everything and refuse to stop harassing her. I think she's slow or something to be honest because Thyri done beat her ass, but she won't stop," she explained.

"That shit is crazy man. She has been through a lot. I mean at this point she might want to get a restraining order or some-thing," Deion replied.

"You don't seem surprised," Kamari replied with a crazy look. She was sure that Thyri hadn't told him all of that. "A restraining order don't mean nothing to that girl."

"Yeah, I heard about that. Was it over on Summit?" Legend asked her. "I heard about that shit though my boy Philly."

"Yup that was him. Crazy as fuck, right?"

"That explains so much. Although she told me a little bit about it, she didn't tell me everything or to this degree. Deion said to them.

"Sorry y'all I need to go to the bathroom," she told them getting up excusing herself.

"Man, I love that woman I can't lose her. I can't even believe I'm saying this shit!" Deion admitted. "I've not even known her that long man."

"She gone be just fine and trust me we know you love her she is all you talk about besides your seed. I feel it though she is dope as fuck. I know you still miss and love Indya and yes this was a fast transition but I'm sure it's real."

"I'm not gone hold you, this shit is scary even for me. I don't want to confuse myself by jumping into this so fast but shit! She got me," he told him. "Not to mention me and Indya haven't resolved our differences."

"Come on, give yourself her a break. You can't control the timing. Shit happens when you least expect it."

"Yeah, I guess. I just got to get her to forgive me for that shit with Alisha. I know that shit was embarrassing to her.

"Aye, I got some Patrón in the truck you want a drink?" Legend asking already knowing the answer.

"Hell yeah, go get that shit."

"Nigga we can't be up in this bitch sipping. I'm going to stop by the vending machine and get a couple of waters and empty them."

"Bet, I'll let Kamari know where you at when she comes back in here."

Deion sat there alone wondering how bad his luck had to be for him to be dealing with this. All he could do was pray for the best. One thing for sure, he wasn't about to leave that hospital until she woke up. Deion wanted badly to call Indya to check on her just because of what he was facing, but he decided against it because she had made her bed so she could lay in it alone.

Although Kamari had let them know that she wasn't in a serious life-threatening situation, he still sent up prayers that her surgery would go well because you could never tell with those things. He knew people that had simple surgeries and they just never woke up...

CHAPTER TWENTY-SEVEN

Mariah finally convinced Indya to go to Greensboro to see exactly what Deion was up to before she made her decision on whether she was going to invite him back home or not. Indya didn't want to call her mother to look after Gianna, but she didn't have a choice in the matter. Her mind was focused on finding out what her man had been up to. The truth was, she missed him like crazy. She thought switching up on him would change his mind on their relationship, but she was wrong. Deion acted as if he was okay with their split. It was time for her to let him see exactly how she got down.

"Hey Ma," Indya greeted when her mother picked up the other end.

"My baby. What's going on?" Pamela quizzed.

"Nothing, I'm going to get Deion and I was wondering if you could keep G.G. until I get back."

"Are you sure that this is what you want? The last time we talked, you didn't want nothing else to do with him. I know you're grown baby, but I need to make sure that you're good. I know that in the past it may have seemed like I was pushing you toward him but in the beginning, I just knew he would make you his wife."

Indya rolled her eyes angrily. She loved her mother, but she wasn't looking for a lecture every time she asked her for advice.

"Mama, I just asked if you could keep Gianna for a few days. Save the lecture. I know you're only looking out for my best interest but some things we must learn on our own," she stated firmly. She loved her mover to no end, but she needed to chill and let her grow up on her own.

"Say no more, Indya," her mother told her saddened by her banter. Pamela wasn't about to argue with her. "I'll keep her for you baby."

"Okay we will be there shortly," Indya replied disconnecting the call.

After packing her daughter, a bag Indya called Mariah to come get her.

"Hello," she answered.

"Hey girl, we're ready whenever you are."

"Okay, bet. I'm on my way I should be there within twenty minutes," she replied disconnecting the call.

Indya wasn't sure what she was going to find out when she got to Greensboro, but she was going to get her man back. she wanted to believe that Deion wasn't doing anything he wasn't supposed to do, but he didn't have such a good track record either. It only made sense that he was up to no good.

In record time Mariah was pulling up tooting her horn for Indya and Gianna to come out.

"Hey girl, my ass is tired," Indya said as she belted her daughter into her seat.

"I know you're not getting nervous?" Mariah quizzed with a raised brow.

"No girl, I'm not going to lie this shit is stressing me out. I mean I know Deion is a whore but for once I hope he's keeping it real with me. I know me not talking to him probably prompted him to fuck some random, but it's time he knows I'm not playing no more games. He will be bringing his ass home."

"I don't know girl. It's hard to say but knowing him he probably is but you can't go out there on demon time because you will be giving him exactly what he is asking for. This man has tried to break you in every way possible and you're still standing. I know you love him Indya but it's time to let it go. If we go out here and he's fuckin' with another bitch leave him there," she urged.

"You don't get it I don't want to hurt my baby. She loves her father to no end and his love for her is unmatched. I just got to see him face to face so we can talk."

"Like I said my girl is going to set us up and we can go from there. I know that I am the one that pushed you to do this, but I don't want to see you hurting again boo. I need you to keep in mind that you've ghosted him for over a month," she told her as they pulled into Pamela's driveway.

"Hold that thought. Let me take her in here," she said getting out the car.

Indya used her spare key to enter the house. When she went inside her mother was cooking dinner with her gospel blasting through the speakers in the kitchen.

"Hey ma," she spoke.

"Give me my baby," she urged holding her arms out.

"Well, hello to you also," she huffed.

"Hey girl, when do you plan on coming back?" she inquired with a scowl on her face. Pamela loved her grandbaby dearly, but she wasn't a fan of her daughter constantly making a fool of herself. She couldn't understand Indya. One minute she was ghosting Deion and the next she was ready to go play private eye to see what he's been up to.

"Don't start ma. I love y'all," she replied kissing her daughter and her mother on the cheek.

"Remember you have a good ass job Indya. Don't go out there acting crazy if you find what you're look for."

"Why are you always so negative? I'm gone ma." She turned around and bolted for the door Indya was not trying to hear nothing her mother was saying. She knew what needed to be done and that's what she was doing.

She hopped in the car and Mariah was on the phone with her friend that they would be going out there to crash with.

"We're on the way," she said disconnecting the call.

"Is everything okay?"

"Yeah, she's waiting for us. She said she got some shit set up so this trip will be worth it. my girl be on her shit," she boasted.

"Good because I can use some downtime before I find out what Deion's ass been up to."

"Aye, what's up with you and Maurice because anyone with eyes can see that he's checking for you."

"Girl, I'm helping him with his case and that's it. Don't get me wrong, I would love to ride that pony, but I'm not trying to lose my job either. That's a big ass conflict of interest. I thought about it though," she admitted, laughing.

"I feel you girl," Mariah replied as they continued their short trip to Greensboro.

Mariah was on the fence. She was still not able to validate her feelings toward Indya, but she damn sure had feelings that she shouldn't have for Deion. The night they all spent together made her fall for him more than she would have liked to, but she couldn't tell her friend that because she didn't want to lose her. In the beginning, what she had with Deion was just a sneaky link every now and then, mostly when he wanted a break away from Indya, but over time her feelings grew. So she just played it off and acted nonchalant when Indya forgave her for creeping with him behind her back...

CHAPTER TWENTY-EIGHT

K amari thought that she would get away from dealing with the police, but as soon as they got a little tipsy off the drink Legend had, a detective came in to ask her some questions. When Kamari saw him walk past the waiting area and head to the nurse's station, she quickly shooed him and Deion off. Knowing what they did, the last thing they needed was for him to be all up in their grills. She grabbed her water and splashed her face so she didn't appear to be as drunk as she was.

"Excuse me, I was told that you came in with Ms. Thyri Jacobs," he spoke. "I have a few questions for you."

"Yes, I did," she replied.

"Do you mind telling me what happened with her and Ms. Francisco?" he asked with his notepad and pen in his hand ready to write. "Now, I do know that they have had problems and some interactions, but I don't know the extent of it."

"Then you know as much as I do because she is crazy. She blamed Thyri for her brother being assaulted, which almost resulted in his death, but that's it," she explained. "That's the story."

"So, you don't know what transpired as to why this happened?"

"Wait, how do you know who shot her?" *Damn, mother-fuckas are running their mouths already,* she thought.

"We received a tip after we got the call about the shooting," he told her.

"Well, I was inside the beauty store when it happened, so I really can't help you, sir."

"Did y'all catch her or what, because I can't take all these questions. If it was her that did this, y'all need to be locking her ass up. She's a menace."

"No, we haven't been able to locate her as of yet, but we are working on it I can assure you that," he informed her.

Thank God, she thought.

"Well, I don't know what to tell you because if I knew where she was, I would be beating her ass!" she barked. "This girl has been a nuisance. I appreciate the information and when my friend wakes up, I'll have her give you a call. Do you have a card?"

"Yes, please have her contact me," he said passing her a business card.

"Thank you, Mr. Williams," she replied as she glanced at his name on the card.

"You have a good rest of your day," he told her as he walked off.

Legend and Deion came waltzing back into the waiting room with breakfast from McDonalds.

"Yesss, I needed this boo," she told Legend. "Ugh this is not how I planned on spending my day, but I'll do anything for my friend."

"You know I got you. We already smashed our shit. We were just waiting for that nigga to leave."

"What did he say?" Deion quizzed.

"You know just asking questions and shit. I barely said much, but he said that they're actively looking for Lamika's ass. Someone already gave them a tip that it was her."

"If they know it was her why the hell are they trying to question y'all that shit don't make no sense," Legend said.

"I have no fuckin' idea. They just need to catch her ass before we do because this bitch done took it too far now."

"I'm just glad nobody at the beauty store told them that Thyri was shooting back at her ass because this would be a whole different conversation. I mean she has a license to carry but they don't give a damn about that shit," she said as she bit into her biscuit. She was starving so that food was hitting the spot.

"I wish she would have hit that hoe because she been on her bully shit and I've seen that shit firsthand," Deion barked.

"You, I wish I was out there I would have shot that goofy my damn self. What's so cold about this shit is that Thyri hasn't even bothered them since her brother got Holyfield. Lamika is pushing the issue because Thyri beat the Sonic coins out of her ass and she's embarrassed."

"Yeah, that bitch mad she got beat that's why she on that type of time now," Legend told her.

"This shit got me hot! I should have been there to protect her man," Deion said chiming into the conversation.

A few minutes later the threesome was given permission to visit with Thyri. She wasn't awake just yet, but they could visit with her.

Deion was the first one to walk into the room and kissed her forehead. Kamari cried she couldn't believe her friend had been shot. The doctor let them know that she would wake up soon and that she was out of the woods.

They each took a seat and began taking to her. Her heart ached with each word that she spoke. The tears were nonstop. They all dropped tears. Legend couldn't believe that it had him all in his feelings but seeing how tore up Kamari was he couldn't help but shed a few tears.

Deion's phone started vibrating in his pocket. He pulled it out his pocked and saw that it was Indya blowing him up. He looked at his phone in disbelief because she wasn't talking to him. The only time they had any communication was when he would call or facetime their daughter.

"I'm sorry y'all I'll be right back I have to take this call," he said excusing himself.

"What is that about?" Kamari asked with a raised brow.

"It's nothing baby. Probably a call about his daughter," he replied.

"Wait, he has a kid? Thyri has never mentioned that to me."

"Yeah, you ain't know? Shit, I thought your girl would have told you."

"Um, no I didn't. Does Thyri even know?" she huffed.

"Yeah, he said she knows about his daughter. Shit you gotta ask her."

"I'm going to kick ya ass." She giggled tapping Thyri's leg.

"I swear y'all have the best relationship."

"I love her so much. We been through everything together," she cried. Legend wrapped his arms around her tightly.

"Hey is everything alright?" he answered.

"Well hello to you also?" Indya huffed.

"I'm sorry but you don't ever call me, so of course I got worried when I saw your name pop up on the screen."

"I was calling to make sure everything is okay. We haven't heard from you. Where are you at?"

"Don't call my phone with no bullshit Indya. Is Gianna, okay?"

"Oh, so now you're worried?"

"I talk to my daughter every day. If I'm not calling you, I'm calling Ms. Pam," he told her.

"Yeah, okay well she hasn't told me nothing about that."

"Take that up with her. Look what are you calling me for man I don't have time to play with you today," he scolded.

"What if I told you I want us to work it out and before you get slick out the mouth, I know that I've been standoffish, but you have to understand my position."

"I would tell you that I don't think I want that anymore. I tried waiting on you to enjoy your space or whatever, but I'm over it, Indya. I love you and always will, but you were right, this has been over for a long time. We have been holding onto something that is no longer there," he honestly spoke.

Indya felt like the wind had been sucked out of her body. She thought that if she put him on punishment for a while, he would see that losing her wasn't worth it, instead she pushed him away.

"I'm not giving up on us Deion. We both have had space to think this over and I'm ready to make it work because I cannot see my life without you in it. I need you. Ginna need you," she said through tears.

Deion just shook his head when he heard her sniffling. She was good for that crying shit when she couldn't have her way.

"Look, kiss my baby girl and tell her that I will call her later," he said disconnecting the call before she could rebut him.

When he walked back into the room Kamari and Legend was about to step out.

"Y'all leaving already?" he asked.

"Yeah, I'm going to run her to the crib so she can get cleaned up," Legend told him. Up until that very second, he hadn't even noticed that she still had blood all over her.

"When we come back you can go home and do what you need to do I know your cold as fuck with them shorts on," Kamari said laughing.

"Hell yeah, but being here with her has taken my mind off it honestly," he said, dapping Legend up and giving Kamari a hug.

Deion sat down and held her hand while he watched her sleep. He had so much to think about. The last thing he wanted to do was to hurt Indya, but he had fallen for Thyri so much so that he was willing to risk it all for her. Never in his life had he met a woman like her. He didn't want to lose her.

"I know you're still mad at me baby. I didn't tell you about Tasty because she meant absolutely nothing to me. I was just in a bad place. I can't take it back though I wish I could. I know I fucked up by not telling you, but I love you so much. Just come back to me Thyri and I will show you just how much I do," he honestly spoke. Just then the nurse came in to check her vitals.

The love that he had for her scared him and he didn't know whether to act on it until the moment Legend told him what had happened.

"Hello, I'm Ms. Jacobs nurse. If you need anything, please let me know. I'm nurse Thorne."

"Yes, ma'am I will thank you. Do y'all have any idea when she might come out of this," he asked.

"We checked her before you all came back, she's heavily medicated so it should be any minute now. Most times it takes at least an hour but it's all up to her sir, we can't tell you exactly when that will happen. I wish we could, but these things take time," she explained.

"Yes, I understand but I had to ask anyway."

"Well again, if you need anything just let me know," she replied as she left the room.

Deion played some soft jazz tunes on his phone and continued to hold her hand. Without even realizing it he started to doze off. He was tired because they hadn't slept at all. Right when he was about to fall deep into his nod, Thyri slightly squeezed his hand. He damn near jumped out his chair.

"Thyri can you hear me. Come on baby get up," he urged. "I'm here, can you hear me."

Deion wanted to press the nurse call button, but he didn't want to jump the gun.

"Can you hear me?" he rubbed her hand and kissed her head. I'm here baby. Come on wake up for me."

The machines started beeping and she squeezed tighter. Thyri eyes slowly opened and blinked rapidly, and her breathing became erratic. Deion freaked out right away.

"Thyri baby are you okay?" he asked pressing the call button over and over until the nurse came running back in her room.

"She's up but I think something is wrong. Help her why are the machines beeping like that? Is she going to be, okay?" Deion was in shambles.

"Nothing is wrong sir, she is probably just in a panic because of where she's at."

Tears fell from Thyri's eyes heavily because Deion was right there with her when she woke up even after she had been pushing him out her life. It meant the world to her that he pushed all of that to the side to be there for her.

Once the nurse removed all the tubes, she paged the doctor on call.

"Ms. Jacobs I'm your nurse, Tina Thorne. Are you feeling alright?" Thyri just shook her head in agreement. She checked her vitals again and asked if she needed anything for pain until she left the room.

"Are you sure that you're, okay?" Deion quizzed.

"Yes, I'm sure," she replied with a wide grin.

"Do you remember what happened?"

"Yes, I remember, and I love you too," she said with a wink. How could she stay mad at him this man was the sweetest thing ever.

"So, you heard me?" he asked shyly. "I didn't know if you would be able to hear me. Kamari and Legend left not too long ago to get cleaned up and shit." He stepped closer and kissed her on her lips.

She sighed heavily as she tried to sit up in the bed. "Ahh," she moaned. "This shit burns."

"Relax baby, you did just get shot." He chuckled.

"Did I hit that bitch and where is my gun?" she asked trying to get up again.

"Please don't try to get up. No, you didn't hit her baby."

"Deion where is my gun?" she demanded.

"Kamari got it before anyone had the chance to get it 12 came by here mad early and questioned her. Matter of fact let me hit Legend so they can pull up," he said shooting him a text.

"I've been so mean to you, Deion. I'm sorry. Why did you come here to check on me?" she inquired.

"I knew that I cared deeply for you. That's why I gave you

space, but when Legend told me that you had been shot, my heart broke and I knew at that very moment that I loved you and I had to be here no matter what you said."

"Help me sit up," she requested. Deion held her hand and placed his right hand on her back to help her.

"Thank you so much for loving me. You have no idea what this means to me, Deion. I didn't think I was worth being loved. Hell, I didn't think I'd ever love someone again, but you have shown me that I am worthy."

"You don't have to thank me, baby. I'm thankful to have found you. Legend just texted and said they're about to pull up."

Deion sat on the bed and held her tightly. He could be like that for a lifetime...

CHAPTER TWENTY-NINE

Thyri couldn't sleep for nothing the night before. She was only focused on getting home and lying in her bed. The amount of love she had for God and the abundance of blessings that he had been bestowing on her recently, all she could do was thank him aloud any chance she got. She was blessed and humbled.

When Kamari came to see her, she brought her phone. The first thing she did was check her social media pages, and there was an unwavering amount of support for her speedy recovery.

It wasn't that she didn't have people show her love daily, but all of this was a bit overwhelming because she couldn't thank everyone. So, she settled on a post. Nothing too long because her arm was still very sore, and it hurt to use it at all.

Deion had kept his word and was there with her for the whole time until she made him go home and get some rest.

Never wanting it to go there, Thyri just wanted her to understand the position she was in when Kane beat her brother. At one time she and Lamar shared something special, so her heart ached for him. One day soon she was going to reach out to him and apologize for everything that happened to him.

Looking down at her phone she began to grow impatient. It

was almost nine a.m. and still no discharge papers. She pressed the nurse call button.

"Um, how much longer do I have to wait for my discharge papers?" she huffed.

"I have them printing off right now, so you can go ahead and call your ride," she told her.

"Ugh, okay thanks." Thyri wanted to snap on her but that would be just downright rude. They had taken such good care of her. She called Kamari soon as the nurse left her room and let her know that she was officially ready to be picked up.

"Hey babes, are you ready?" she asked excitingly.

"Girl, hell yeah. Come get me. Ugh, I just want to lay in my bed and sleep for a week," she said laughing.

"Well, we're on the way," Kamari replied.

"What you mean? We?" Thyri inquired. The plan was for Kamari to come get her.

"Don't trip. I'll call you when we about to pull up because I know they not about to let you walk down by yourself."

"If you say so boo. Just hurry up. I'm in desperate need of something other than hospital food."

"Okay, I love you girl."

"I love you too, Kamari," she said disconnecting the call.

As promised the nurse came right back into her room with her discharge papers in hand.

"See that wasn't so bad now, was it?"

"No ma'am and please forgive me for being short with you earlier. I apologize. I want to personally thank you for helping me get back on my feet."

"It's no worries love and you're very welcome. I know how it can be no one wants to be in the hospital for any period. Just make sure you take care of yourself young lady," she told her.

"Well, you all are appreciated," Thyri told her.

"Absolutely no worries. Now are you ready to get out of here?"

"My friend is on her way so if it's not too much can you take me down now, so she doesn't have to wait?"

"No problem. Are you taking all your flowers and things." Thyri turned and looked at everything and smiled.

"No, I'm sure you can find someone in need of a little bit of love."

The moment the elevator doors opened Kamari was standing there with the biggest smile on her face.

"Hey bitch!" she said bending down kissing and hugging Thyri.

"Ouch, not too tight boo. You got here fast as hell."

"Oh shit, I got too excited. I'm just glad you're coming home I don't know what I would have done if you didn't make it, girl. Thank you, I can take it from here," Kamari said, helping her out the wheelchair. "I told Deion you were ready to be released and that fool broke records getting us here."

She helped Thyri walk over to Deion's new SUV. "I see Legend got something new," she said.

"Nah, this is Deion's shit girl. I just told you he drove girl." Kamari giggled.

Thyri was in awe. She knew he was making money with Legend, but she didn't think enough to cop a 2023 G-wagon.

"Bitch why you ain't tell me?"

"Because it wasn't for me to tell," she said as they got closer to the truck.

"Here, I got her," Deion said jumping out the driver's seat to help her inside.

"Umph, excuse me," Kamari said jokingly.

"Thank you, baby," she flirted.

"I got you," he told her with a wink. "You want to go out and get something to eat? I got us a table reserved at Undercurrent Restaurant," Deion told her.

"Awe, y'all are really the best. I can't believe that God sent y'all to me, but I hate to break it to ya, but I'm still in a lot of pain. I just want to go home and relax, guys. Please don't be mad at me."

"Damn Thyri, I wasn't even thinking," Kamari apologized.

"Yeah, it wasn't intentional at all," Legend said.

"That's so selfish of us ,man. To be honest, I wasn't thinking at all. Nobody is mad, shorty. You have a point," Deion told her.

"It's okay, y'all don't have to beat yourselves up. What if we just have a staycation at my crib and order in?" she offered.

"That sounds good too. Shit, I like that idea better," Deion replied. Thyri just shook her head.

"Are you sure?" Kamari asked her. "Does he know about your new spot?"

"No, so it will be like that housewarming you were trying to get me to agree to have before all of this shit happened." She giggled.

"Oh, you're heading in the wrong direction baby," she told him.

"You moved?" Deion quizzed and he and Legend looked at each other.

"Yes, I moved," she said telling him which direction to head in.

"I see we have a lot to catch up on," he replied.

"I agree Mr. new whip," she said laughing.

"You gonna just let her come for your neck like that?" Legend teased.

"It's all good. She knows what it is," he replied. Thyri and Kamari were in the back seat cracking up.

The way their mouths dropped when they made it to her house said everything without them uttering a word.

"Damn baby, this is you for real?" Deion quizzed with a raised brow. This was a drastic jump from her condo.

"Yup, she is all mine," she happily replied. "Damn, look at all of these packages." The last thing that was on her mind was everything being delivered while she was laid up in the hospital.

"Let me find out you the plug or some shit. Ain't no way you went from that condo to this in a month," Legend said.

"What the hell is that supposed to mean?" Kamari snapped.

"Chill bae, you know I didn't mean it like that. It just came out wrong," Legend told her. "My bad Thyri."

"Man, you are good. My girl just being a little sensitive. You know she's super overprotective over me."

Deion put his truck in park and helped Thyri to the front door.

"Come here, Kamari, help her. We got the bags and shit, and these packages. Damn girl, what did you do, order everything from Amazon?" Legend said as they disappeared through the doors.

Soon as they were out of sight, Legend punched Deion in the arm.

"Nigga, where do you think she got the money for a spot like this?"

"Your guess is as good as mine, but I'm sure she will let me know, and as soon as she does, you'll be the first to know."

"All I'm going to say is don't blow shit this time around."

"Fuck you, nigga, you know damn well that first little situation was out of my hands," Deion told him.

"Yeah, well just don't do it again," he warned. "Can't find a bitch out here with their own shit."

"Trust me, I ain't on none of that shit. She gone make a playa change his ways."

"Yeah, that's if Indya don't kill your ass first," he said jokingly.

Deion's head was turning in so many directions he couldn't keep up. He knew that this little staycation would be the perfect time for them to clear the air and lay it all down. That love word falling off their lips said so...

CHAPTER THIRTY

"Baby, you got this shit set up nice," Deion complimented as they walked into her house.

"Man, this is a come up, for real. I know you're happy to be out the hood, huh?" Legend spoke.

"Y'all have no idea. And to clear the air, I got this from a settlement so to speak. I don't move no work or nothing like that." She giggled.

"If you say so, but this is most definitely giving plug vibes," Legend said, clowning.

"Y'all know damn well she ain't on no hot shit like that," Kamari replied.

"Can we get a tour though?" Deion said, putting his arm around her waist.

"My girl got y'all. I'm not about to hit them stairs right now," she told them. "And please don't be weird. Y'all can relax like it's your own spot. This is the only circle that knows where I live," she explained, just in case they had their reservations. She let Kamari show them around because she wanted to make her phone call in peace.

As Kamari took them on a tour of her house, Thyri used that time to contact her social worker, Samantha. She had a visit already set in motion to take place in three more days. The last thing she needed was for her to find out about her being shot. Thyri was sure that would be an issue, but then she wanted to be certain.

"This is Samantha," she answered.

"Hey Mrs. Johnson, it's Thyri. I wanted to touch bases and make sure that my visit would still be this Thursday," she spoke politely.

"Give me just a minute, let me double check," she replied.

"Well, that's the day that you told me," Thyri huffed, slightly annoyed.

"I know, honey, I just got to make sure. I'm checking my calendar. Give me a few minutes," she replied, placing Thyri on a brief hold.

Thyri was biting her bottom lip, shaking her leg, annoyed with this woman. She silently prayed that nothing had changed. Her heart was set on seeing her babies when promised. There was no room in her life for error. This would most definitely fuck her up if she couldn't see them.

"Okay, yes, I have it and we will see you Thursday, Ms. Jacobs," she told her.

This bitch must really think I'm stupid. She knows damn well the day she told me, she thought.

"Okay, thank you, bye," she said, disconnecting the call just in time because Kamari and the guys just walked back in the house.

"Man, this shit is nice as fuck. You did good with this one right here," Legend told her.

"Hell yeah, and the fact that you have a pool and lake on the property is fire as fuck," Deion spoke.

"Thank y'all so much. Legend, you got a nice house too," she replied.

"Wait until you see Deion's shit," Legend blurted out, not realizing that she didn't know about it yet.

"Not you got a house too. You're just full of surprises, I see. Anyway, y'all hungry? Because I'm starving."

"Hell yeah," they all said in unison.

"It's just a little condo, nothing too crazy. I wanted to tell you, but you weren't talking to me, remember?" Deion told her.

"Oh yeah, I forgot about that," she said, laughing. "I can't have any, but I have a full selection of drinks in the pantry if y'all want some." Thyri knew she couldn't drink because of all the meds she was on, but she wanted her friends to enjoy themselves.

"Shit, let's do this," Kamari said, going to grab a bottle for them.

"If you're not drinking baby, I know you want to smoke," Deion spoke with a smile.

"Hell yeah, so roll something up, boo." As badly as she wanted to drink, she couldn't because she didn't want to get an infection or go back to the hospital. That was the last place she wanted to see again. After her two-day stay, that was enough to last her a lifetime.

"Yo, let's play drunk UNO. You can just take shots of juice or something, boo," Kamari told Thyri.

Legend looked down at his phone and saw that he had mad missed calls from Rocky and Philly, but he just powered his phone off.

"These niggas been blowing my shit down," he complained.

"Probably some groupies blowing you down nigga," Kamari spat. "Tell 'em I got your ass for the next couple of days."

"Knock it off girl. You know better than that," he replied.

"Them nigga's needy as fuck man. Don't even let them know where we are," Deion told him.

"I'm just gone tell them niggas know we're out the city on business or something. Knowing them fools they'll want to put up and chop it up if they know I'm here."

"Yeah, that ain't happening at all. They're weirdos and they don't need to know where Thyri lays her head," Kamari told him.

"I know, and I got this, baby," Legend replied.

Thyri got up off the couch and went up to her room so she could put something more comfortable on. The jeans that Kamari brought her to the hospital weren't cutting it any longer. Sweats and a t-shirt were the move.

"Are you okay? You need some help?" Deion asked, jumping to his feet.

"No, I'm okay, and I need to move around so that I heal faster. Sitting around won't do nothing for me boo. Sit down and relax, I'll be okay. I promise you I got this." She giggled.

Deion couldn't wait until she felt better. He hated that he couldn't be there to protect her. Although she hadn't shared too much with him about her life, he knew that she deserved better than what she had been through...

CHAPTER THIRTY-ONE

The evening approached quickly with heavy rain and thunderstorms. They were all faded, having a blast.

"Y'all, I can't hang. I'm about to go upstairs and take it down," she announced.

"I don't think I could have said it better," Deion said, standing up.

"Y'all are party poopers," Kamari said.

"Girl, I'm off these meds and the weed didn't help at all. I can't wait to lay in my bed."

"Don't worry about us. I'm sure we can find something to do," Legend said, licking his lips.

"Here you go," she replied.

"Goodnight you two, don't do nothing we wouldn't do," Thyri teased as they made their way upstairs.

"Oh, you know I will," Kamari said laughing.

"No fuckin' on my couch, heffa. Take your ass to one of the spare bedrooms!"

When they got into the bedroom, Deion helped Thyri into the shower. He was doing whatever he could to cater to her needs.

Deion bathed her and made sure to wash every inch of her body. Thyri never had anyone to love on her so much. The way he caressed her body sent chills up her spine. Once their shower was over, they headed back to the room.

"Thank you so much Deion. I was terrible to you, and you still showed up for me that means the world to me. No one has shown up for me like that but my girl."

"I don't know what it is about you Thyri but I just want to be here for you. Speaking of which, I think now is good a time as any for us to talk about what's been going on. I don't want us to keep anything from each other anymore. I know that this wasn't official before, but I want this more than you know. So, if you'll have me, I want us to be official. I don't ever want to lose you. Like riding down the street with the windows down, official." He chuckled. Deion planned on letting Indya know that he was moving to Greensboro and what they had was over.

"If I will have you," she said, cracking up laughing. "This ain't the '80s boo. Of course, I'll have you," she replied.

"Look, don't be laughing at me."

"I couldn't help it you walked into that one bae."

"Nah, but for real, I think that if we're going to be together, we must be honest with each other. I mean I told you that shit was basically complicated with me and my daughter's mother. Well, I'm going to end it with her because this is where I want to be."

"Deion, I don't know what to say to that. I mean I'm flattered but I don't want to come in between you two."

"You're not coming in between anything. I told you that what we had has been over for a while. It has nothing to do with you, so you have nothing to worry about."

"I don't know her but I'm sure she isn't going to just be okay with this decision. I just don't need no drama in my life," she honestly spoke.

"Listen to me, the last thing I would do is bring drama to you baby. I will make sure that she understands that this is what I want. I got you Thyri."

"Yeah, I get it baby." Ahem, she cleared her throat. "Are you sure you're ready for all the bullshit I think you should know? I don't even like victimizing myself but it's important that you know everything."

"I'm sure it's not all that bad," he replied. "We all have a past baby."

"Look it's a lot so if you want to run now, I'll understand," she told him laughing uneasily.

"I'm not going anywhere," he told her putting his arms around her. "You aren't getting away from me that easy."

"I honestly don't even know where to start." She sighed heavily.

"So, when I was like thirteen my parents were killed in a fatal car accident. Luckily, I got away with a few scrapes and bruises. I went into the foster care system. That's where I met Alisha or Tasty. She had a similar story to mine, so I took to her. Anyway, I fell in love with who I thought was the love of my life. He showed me his love through his fists. For a long time, I thought it was love. Until I had enough and then it was like torture, but I loved him," she continued. "I thought I was rid of him, but I wasn't. I watched him beat the shit out of a guy that I was with. Mind you he and I was no longer together. I even had an active restraining order on him, but that still didn't keep him away." She cried. "He just couldn't take that I no longer wanted to be with him."

"It's okay, you don't have to keep going. I understand baby."

"No, I need to get this out. Kamari is the only one that knows. Maybe talking it out will help me heal. Thank you, bae."

"I got you. Don't even worry about it."

"I don't even like saying his name anymore, but after he beat my friend, he kidnapped me and took me to a hotel out in High Point. I don't know where the courage came from, but I waited for him to go to sleep, and I got the hell out of there and didn't look back. I don't know if it was the coke or cockiness, but he thought I was going to stay there with him for whatever reason. Thankfully his crazy ass is locked up. I truly hope they never let him go. I'm glad that I moved because if he does get out, he won't know where to find me."

"Shit, you been through some rough stuff baby, but you made it out. You're beating the odds. And won't nobody else put their hands on you. I promise you that."

"I do feel safe in your arms," she flirted. "There is more though, Deion. You know I have kids; I have three. I lost custody because of all the abuse. You sure you don't want to run?" she asked before finishing her story.

Deion was taken aback. His mouth hit the floor. At first, he didn't know how to respond.

"I'm not going anywhere girl, so stop. I didn't expect you to say you have three kids, but it's going to take a helluva lot more than kids to run me off. I love kids, baby. I told you I always wanted at least ten."

"Whoa, hold your horses, buddy. I'm not pushing out no damn ten kids. Well, six more kids." She laughed. "Although I hate their father for what he took me through, my kids are my everything. I'm trying to get them back now. If it wasn't for him, I wouldn't have this house. He kept his grandmother's ring at my house after I rejected his proposal, and that shit was worth a grip. I figured that was the least he could do since he was the reason I lost my babies. Okay, that's it, bae. My dirty little secrets. I just want to put that part of my life behind me and move forward, you know?"

"I don't know, I think it's kind of poetic that we met. I guess we were what the other one needed. I'm glad I found you," he said, pressing his lips against hers and kissing her.

"Well, I think I found you that night we were in the club. Remember, it was us that sent y'all some food," she teased.

"Touché, baby."

Thyri felt so much better now that she was able to tell him everything that she had been hiding from him. A weight had been lifted from her shoulders...

CHAPTER THIRTY-TWO

The next morning, Thyri was feeling a lot better. When she rolled over and looked at her phone, she had a ton of notifications. That was her new norm, and she didn't care for it at all. She went straight to Lamika's page and there was an overwhelming number of posts talking about how she led the police on a high-speed chase before getting caught. It blew her that they were all tagging Lamika. As crazy as it may have seemed, Thyri felt bad for her in some way. She didn't quite know why she felt pity for the person who made it their mission to ruin her life, but she did.

After she finished checking her socials, she headed to the kitchen. Everyone was still sound asleep.

I know these niggas about to wake up starved, she thought as she pulled food from the fridge. Her shoulder throbbed like hell, but she was able to push through by only using her other arm. Of course, she kept taking breaks, but she made it through. Since she was basically hosting this little staycation, it was only right that she cooked for them.

"Girl, what are you doing? What time is it?" Kamari said, rubbing her eyes as she walked in the kitchen.

"Well, you're glowing." She giggled. "I know what your freaky ass was doing last night."

"Shut up. Why the hell are you trying to cook girl? I know your arm is on fire."

"No, not really. I took my pills this morning. I ain't feeling no pain, boo."

"I'm low-key glad you did cook, because I'm hungry," she said, walking to the fridge to get a bottle of water. "I swear after a night of drinking, I'm parched like a motherfucka."

"Man, don't I know it. I can drink the whole city's water supply when I have a hangover."

"Deion about to wake up in heaven."

"You act like he's never tasted my cooking before. He's going to love it here," she said, twisting around in a circle. "Ouch, shit."

"You better stop. You act like you didn't get shot a couple of days ago, but I can't front I am so happy for how you've turned your life around. I know everyone probably counted you out, but I always believed in you."

"Thank you, but it wouldn't have been possible without you in my corner. Having someone like you has made life so much easier. And I told Deion everything last night. You know how chatty I get when I'm high."

"You know I'm never going anywhere girl. And it's about time you told him. I know it was killing you not to let him know from jump, but I think everything happened in God's timing boo."

"I guess. Just wish a bitch didn't have to get shot the fuck up first." Thyri said making light of the situation. She pulled the crescent rolls from the oven and covered them with butter and honey.

"I'm about to fuck that shit up. It all smells so good boo."

"Me too. I think I still got the munchies from last night or something. That's probably why the first thing on my mind was food. Can you go wake your man's up. Send him upstairs to get Deion too because I don't feel like climbing them steps."

"Hey, y'all come eat!" Kamari yelled from the bottom of the stairs.

"You really ain't shit. I could have done that. I swear you're so annoying," Thyri complained.

"Whatever, say what you will, but it works boo. Watch how quick they be down here. Damn, maybe I shouldn't have done that. Now my head is hurting."

"I know better next time and that's what you get," she teased as she finished up making their plates. She made waffles, bacon, eggs, sausage, and some home fries.

"Why the hell are you yelling like a wild banshee girl," Legend said in a low whisper. "Oh, y'all done came down here and got down."

"Thyri's cripple ass did all of this. I woke up to this as well babe," Kamari told him.

"Where the hell is Deion?" she huffed.

"I'm right here baby?" he said coming into the kitchen pulling his wife beater over his head.

"I was wondering what you were doing," she said passing him his plate.

"I had to take a piss before I came down here. You didn't have to do this we could have gone and got something. I know you're in pain," he replied.

"Y'all gone need to quit acting like I'm going to break. Thank y'all for being worried but I promise I am just fine," she huffed.

"Okay, my bad," he said kissing her lips.

They all grabbed their plates and went to the dining area.

"So, what are we doing today?" Legend asked cramming eggs down his throat.

"It really isn't a whole lot that we can do," Kamari replied.

"I wish it was hot outside because we could kick it by the pool," Thyri replied.

Soon after Legend's phone went off and wouldn't stop. If looks could kill his ass would have been dead on the spot the way Kamari was side eyeing him.

"Yo," he answered. His face dropped and he sprang from his seat.

"What's going on?" Deion quizzed.

"That was Casha calling me from some lady's phone. She out at Lander's supermarket off West Wendover. Something about an active shooter," he said as he darted to the back of the house to retrieve his pants.

"Oh my God, are they alright?" Thyri asked in a panic.

"I don't know but I have to get there," he replied.

"I hope they're alright," Kamari said. How could she not feel for him.

Deion rushed upstairs and grabbed his keys and ran straight back down them and out the door so fast they didn't even have time to give a proper goodbye.

"This shit is so crazy these days. What goes through someone's head to make them want to kill innocent strangers? Thyri said going in the living room and turning the news on.

"I don't know, that's why I don't like being in those settings. Shit, at the club niggas can't get their straps in that bitch, but a grocery store, you can bring whatever."

Legend was a nervous wreck as they drove at record breaking speeds to get there. When they got close, they had to park and walk the rest of the way because the police presence was so heavy. He didn't know what to do when they wouldn't let him get too close, so they ducked off to the other side.

When they got closer, they saw a body lying on the ground covered up with a rifle beside him.

"I'm glad they caught that nigga," Deion said. Legend didn't even hear him saying shit his ears were on mute until he saw Casha and the twins at an ambulance.

"Hey, y'all good?" he asked her.

"She good my boy. I got her taken care of," the muscular guy on side of the ambulance said.

"Who the fuck is this clown ass nigga Casha?" he barked.

Legend didn't care who was putting it to his baby's mother, but he wasn't about to play with this nigga either.

"Come on man 12 is hot as fish grease out here don't do this right now. We came for your babies," Deion told him.

"Yes, please can y'all not do this right now," she huffed.

Legend grabbed his girls from her arms and held them tight as he could. "Man was y'all in the store?"

"No, we had just walked outside, and that motherfucker bumped me and when I realized that he had a gun I damn near broke my legs getting to the car."

"Thank God y'all are okay I don't know what I would have done if I lost y'all man."

"My nerves are shot," she cried. Her first instinct was to lay in his arms, but she had to quickly pull away because her new man was there, and she didn't want them to be on that type of time.

"Y'all good now, don't cry man." Deion just stood there being supportive to his friend. He knew Casha couldn't stand him. Although she had no reason to be like that to him, he wasn't about to force anything with her.

"Thank you for coming too, Deion," she said, giving him a hug. He almost didn't know how to receive her, but he knew she must have been scared for her life.

"It's no problem. I'm glad y'all good though. This shit is wicked. I always hear about this shit, but to nearly witness it is something else." Deion didn't know who this cat was that was with her, but he wasn't about to take his eyes off him because he was acting sketchy as hell.

"You want me to take the girls with me?" Legend asked her.

"No, I just want to be with my babies. That bastard killed seven people, and for what?" she said, crying again. Her emotions were all over the place.

They stayed there until Casha spoke to the police and headed on their way. Legend felt so much better knowing that they were safe...

CHAPTER THIRTY-THREE

The next day, their staycation was over, and it was time for everyone to leave and go about their way.

"Bae, what you think about coming over one day soon to see my new spot?"

"Do you think that's a good idea? I mean, I don't want to run into your BM while I'm there."

"She doesn't know where I live baby, but I get it. I need to handle that first," Deion said, kissing Thyri passionately.

"That sounds good to me, baby." She smiled.

"Alright now, wrap it up," Kamari told them.

Thyri turned around and gave her the middle finger.

Once everyone cleared out. Thyri put her playlist on her surround sound throughout the house, cracked her laptop open, and checked on her shipments that were still in transit. She was ready to heal so she could open her business. That was one thing she kept from Deion. She would tell him that once she opened.

Although she wanted to let him know about her new business ventures, she didn't want to jinx anything by speaking too fast. Yes, everything was all in motion, but she just wanted to be sure. Two more days and she would be able to see her babies. She was so excited because she hadn't seen them in almost a year, and her baby when she was born.

Thyri went on her Facespace page and created herself a business page. She posted all the pictures that she had in her phone of the entire process. Some pictures of hair and other things she was going to sell. After she finished, she just started sharing it to her page and invited people from her friend's list. She was hoping that everyone would support her new venture, but she also knew how people could be when it came to supporting black-owned businesses.

Deion dropped Legend off and headed home and called Indya but she didn't answer. He ended up calling her mother to see where she was.

"Hello," Pamela answered.

"Hey Ms. Pam, is Indya around? I tried calling her, but she isn't answering."

After a long pause she finally replied to him. "I wasn't going to say anything because I didn't want to get into y'all's business, but she is in Greensboro. She been there for a couple of days. She hasn't reached out to you?" she probed.

"Nah, she ain't told me shit," he replied. "What is she doing out here?"

"All I know is that she said she was coming to get you, so I don't know why she hasn't said anything."

"Alright, if she calls don't let her know that I reached out. I gotta go," he said, shaking his head. He couldn't believe she was trying to pop up on him. He figured that's why she called trying to reconcile with him.

After disconnecting the call, Deion paced the floor and tried calling Indya back several more times to no avail.

This girl done lost her damn mind, he thought. He was fuming.

After Deion tried calling her, Legend called and told him to get ready. Without any questions, Deion did what was asked of him.

"Wassup my boy? What's going on?" Deion asked as he climbed into his SUV. He wanted to tell him about the stunt Indya had just pulled, but he wanted to be sure.

"Not shit, nigga. I wanted to pull up on Rocky and Philly over at the pool hall and see what they got going on.

"I'm with it, but I swear if that nigga Rocky on bullshit, I'm gonna smack him. I know that nigga not on me like that, but the disrespect is something I won't keep tolerating," Deion warned.

"Rocky cool he can be a little belligerent but he's cool. Y'all just not seeing eye to eye right now. Niggas will get over that shit," Legend told him.

"I hear you but I ain't fuckin' with his ass. I know that's your boy and shit but I'm good on him."

"I feel you he can be a little bit too much sometimes," Legend agreed as he bumped his music on the loudest setting.

Legend could relate to Deion because when he and Rocky first got cool, he almost went upside his head a few times too because he has a slick ass tongue.

When they got to the pool hall, Rocky and Philly was going at it over a game.

"Do y'all niggas ever get tired?" Legend asked as they approached them.

"This nigga is just mad I'm kicking his ass! I don't know why he insists on playing me for money," Philly barked.

"This motherfucka be cheating!" Rocky snapped.

"How the hell can I cheat at pool nigga? Make it make sense," Philly taunted. "Just run me my bread."

"Rack them motherfuckas up. Let's play Deion," Legend said. Up until that point Rocky hadn't even noticed him.

"The fuck this nigga doing here?" he barked.

"I don't know what you on Rocky, but it won't be too much more of that disrespectful shit!" Deion said, gritting his teeth.

"Damn, you fuckin' this nigga's bitch or something? Because he been on ya top, Deion," Philly said.

"I'on know what his issue is for real. He's on some hating shit.

Nigga is mad I make more bread than him," Deion barked angrily.

Rocky didn't have a clear chance in hell to rebut Deion because next thing they knew, all hell was breaking loose when Marisha ran up on Philly and started banging him in the head, screaming and crying. She caught all of them off guard.

"You son of a bitch! You gave me HIV! How could you do this to me, to the baby I'm carrying!" she cried.

"Bitch, don't come up in here lying on me! I'll kill you for some shit like that! I don't got no fuckin' HIV!" he shouted.

"Fuckin' all of them nasty ass bitches, now I have to live with this shit for the rest of my life!" she yelled, kicking wildly as Rocky lifted her off her feet.

Deion and Legend looked straight at each other, floored. Deion observed the room, and everyone had their phones out recording.

"Put that shit down. This not the viral moment you mother-fuckers looking for!" Philly shouted, running up on one guy and slapping his phone from his hand.

"Come on," Deion said, trying to usher her out the building. "Y'all need to talk about this in private."

"Fuck that, this nigga out here with that hot shit fuckin' everything walking! That's attempted murder!" she cried, rushing him again.

"Man, come on, y'all are tweaking out! Take that shit outside, niggas recording and shit! Y'all about to go viral for sure," Legend said, using his coat to cover his face.

"I knew that nigga had something going on." Rocky laughed. "Nigga stayed fuckin' them stripper bitches! You might want to get checked, Deion."

"Y'all got to get the fuck out my spot with this shit!" the owner shouted as he walked over to them with his shotgun in hand.

"Damn, you gone shoot us Paul?" Deion quizzed, putting his hand on his strap.

"Don't even think about it, nigga! Y'all always have something going on when y'all come here. It's time to go!"

Philly grabbed Marisha by her knotless braids and drug her out the pool hall. "Let's go, bitch! You wanted some attention, now you have it."

"Ayo, Philly, chill out with that," Deion said, running up behind him. "They're recording this shit!"

"Get this lying ass hoe out my face before I catch a case," he barked, getting into his car and speeding off.

"Are you okay?" Deion asked her.

"Get the fuck off me, nigga! Y'all probably knew he had that shit," she huffed, walking away.

"Well damn, I was just trying to help," Deion said, laughing it off.

"That bitch is crazy! I don't doubt what she's saying though, because Philly dipped like that. Shit wicked, man," Legend told them.

"Everybody and their mammy know that nigga nasty as fuck. I'm not surprised he got that hot shit!" Rocky said. "Anyway, Legend, what's up nigga? I tried hitting you up and shit. I had some money to make and couldn't because you ghosted me."

Everyone that was inside the pool hall was now outside recording and laughing. Their socials were about to be on fire. Philly would have to go dark for a while if he wanted to hide from this.

"Man, shit, something came up. I got some other shit going on with this new connect. I gotta head his way to meet up and then I can throw y'all something. Shit just dry right now," Legend told him. What little bit he had left was going in his and Deion's pocket.

"What that mean? I need to make some bread, nigga," Rocky barked.

"Watch who you're talking to, Rocky. I got y'all but I need a week so I can get this shit together."

Deion just walked off and got back in the whip because he

had enough of Rocky, and they would be the next thing mother-fuckas recorded if he uttered another word to him. That was for Legend to handle anyway...

To Be Continued

Printed in the USA
CPSIA information can be obtained
at www.ICGtesting.com
LVHW040626020424
776092LV00021B/84